CW01643512

Granny's Ghost and the Bake Off Bribe

Ghostly Gumshoe Cozy Mysteries Series, Volume 3

Sloane Finley

Published by Ginger and Spice Publishing, 2025.

This is a work of fiction. Similarities to real people, places, or events are entirely coincidental.

GRANNY'S GHOST AND THE BAKE OFF BRIBE

First edition. July 11, 2025.

Copyright © 2025 Sloane Finley.

ISBN: 979-8231003006

Written by Sloane Finley.

Table of Contents

Chapter 1

I stand in front of my closet, my heart pounding like a drum in my chest. The clothes hanging in front of me seem to mock my indecision, each dress, top, and skirt a potential disaster waiting to happen. My hands hover uncertainly between a sunny yellow sundress and a more sophisticated navy blue blouse. "Come on, Lena," I mutter to myself, "it's just a date. You've solved murders, for crying out loud. You can handle this."

But can I? I've known Mark as the town sheriff, as a colleague—and sometimes obstacle—in solving crimes, but never like this. Never as a potential... what? Boyfriend? The word feels strange, almost foreign in my mind.

I close my eyes, letting my mind wander back to our last conversation. We were standing right inside my front door. Mark had been shuffling his feet, his usually confident demeanor replaced by an endearing nervousness.

"Well," he began, "I was hoping that now things have died down a bit, you might consider... that is, if you're interested... maybe we could go out to dinner sometime?"

The memory of how my heart had leaped into my throat still makes my stomach flutter. I'd managed to stammer out a "yes" without making a complete fool of myself, but now, faced with the reality of our impending date, I'm not so sure about my composure.

At least I convinced him that the annual New Oslo Bake-Off would be the best place for our date, and I'm glad I did. First, I'm the kind of girl who doesn't mind a little dessert for dinner, and the bake-off is sure to have all the best, freshest, most delicious desserts within the city limits.

And second? The festival passes right in front of my house. We won't even have to drive anywhere.

Through my bedroom window, I can hear the bustling sounds of the bake-off being set up right now. The festival stretches all the way down Main Street, and it has always been a tradition in my family to come here, to my Granny Ingrid's house, and have tea before we visit the bake-off.

That was before Granny passed away, though. I wonder if she'll want to keep that tradition going now that she's a ghost. I also wonder if—

"Oh, for the love of all that's holy and unholy, Lena! Just pick something already!"

I nearly jump out of my skin at the sudden intrusion, whirling around to find Granny Ingrid's ghostly form floating near my bed. Her arms are crossed, and she's wearing that exasperated expression I remember so well from my childhood—the one that says she's about two seconds away from taking matters into her own spectral hands.

"Granny!" I exclaim, my hand flying to my chest. "You scared me half to death!"

She raises an eyebrow, a mischievous glint in her otherworldly eyes. "Well, considering I'm already fully dead, I'd say you're still doing better than me, dear." Her transparent form glides over to the closet, passing right through me and sending a shiver down my spine. "Now, let's see what we've got here. Hmm... no, too frumpy... too revealing... oh, honey, burn this one..."

I watch, torn between amusement and mortification, as my grandmother's ghost rifles through my wardrobe. "Granny, I can dress myself, you know. I'm not a child anymore."

She turns to me, hands on her hips. "Could have fooled me, the way you've been dithering about. Now, listen here, Lena. You're going on a date with a handsome man who's seen you elbow-deep in murder investigations. I think we're well past the point of playing coy."

I feel my cheeks flush. "It's not that simple, Granny. Mark and I... well, we've always had a professional relationship. This is different."

"Different?" Granny Ingrid scoffs, turning back to the closet. "Aha! This is the one." She points to a emerald green wrap dress I'd forgotten I owned. "It brings out your eyes, shows off your figure without being too much, and it's comfortable enough for a stroll through the bake-off."

I pull out the dress, holding it up against myself. "Are you sure? It's not too... I don't know, bold?"

Granny Ingrid floats over to me, her spectral hand coming to rest on my shoulder. I can't feel it, not really, but there's a comforting coolness where she touches me. "Lena, my dear, you are a smart, beautiful woman who's faced down killers and unraveled mysteries. It's time you showed the world—and Mark—just how magnificent you are."

Before I can respond, there's a knock at the door, followed by the sound of it swinging open. "Yoo-hoo! Fashion emergency response team, reporting for duty!"

Charlie bursts into the room, her arms laden with bags that clink suspiciously. She's already dressed for the bake-off, wearing a cute apron over her clothes with "Charlie's Chunky Chocolate Chip Champs" emblazoned across the front.

"Charlie!" I exclaim, grateful for the distraction. "I thought you'd be setting up your booth by now."

She grins, dumping her bags onto my bed. An assortment of chocolates, chips, and what looks suspiciously like a bottle of wine spill out. "Are you kidding? This is way more important. Besides, I've got time. My booth is right across the street, remember? Perks of being your bestie."

I can't help but smile as I watch her rummage through the snacks. "You're a lifesaver, Charlie. I don't know what I'd do without you."

"Starve, probably," she quips, tossing me a chocolate bar. "Now, let's talk strategy."

I frown, unwrapping the chocolate. "Strategy? It's a date, not a military operation."

Charlie wags a finger at me. "Every date is a military operation, my friend. We need to plan for all contingencies." She pulls out her phone, waving it at me. "I've got my finger on the trigger, ready to call with a fake emergency if you need an out. One text from you, and bam! Sudden case of food poisoning from some bad rhubarb pie."

I can't help but laugh. "Charlie, I'm not going to fake food poisoning to get out of a date with Mark."

She shrugs, popping a chip into her mouth. "We'll see. The offer stands, though. Just in case."

As I slip on the dress Granny suggested, I catch sight of myself in the mirror. The woman staring back at me looks... different. Confident, maybe? Or at least, less terrified than I feel inside.

Charlie appears behind me, resting her chin on my shoulder. "You look amazing, Lena," she says softly. "Mark's not going to know what hit him."

I take a deep breath, letting it out slowly. "Thanks, Charlie. For everything."

She grins, giving me a quick hug. "That's what friends are for, right? Now, I've got to run and set up my booth. But I'll be keeping an eye out, okay? If you need anything—a pep talk, a distraction, or a getaway vehicle—I'm your girl."

As Charlie heads out, her departure seems to signal a shift in the atmosphere. The excited bustle from the street below grows louder, and I can hear people laughing and calling out to each other as they set up their booths. The festival is coming to life, and with it, the reality of my impending date.

I turn back to the mirror, smoothing down the fabric of my dress. A mix of emotions swirls within me—excitement, nervousness, and a tinge of uncertainty that I can't quite shake. It's been so long since I've been on a date. And Mark... well, he's not just anyone. He's the sheriff, someone I've worked with to solve crimes. Someone who's seen me at my best and my worst.

"You've got this, Lena," I whisper to myself, tucking a strand of hair behind my ear. "You're a strong, capable woman. You've faced down murderers, for heaven's sake. You can handle a date."

But can I? The doubt creeps in, insidious and familiar. What if I say the wrong thing? What if we have nothing to talk about? What if this changes everything between us, and not for the better?

I shake my head, trying to dispel the negative thoughts. This isn't just about me, I realize. It's about Mark, too. He's probably just as nervous, just as uncertain. The thought is oddly comforting.

As I make my way downstairs, I can feel Granny Ingrid's presence following me. I'm pretty sure I can even catch the scent of her favorite perfume wafting through the air from time to time.

I pause at the front door, my hand on the knob. Through the window, I can see the colorful booths lining Main Street, the festive banners fluttering in the breeze. Somewhere out there, Mark is waiting for me. The thought sends a thrill of anticipation through me.

"Well, go on then," Granny Ingrid's voice comes from behind me. "Your man isn't going to wait all day."

I turn to see her materialize in the hallway, a proud smile on her transparent face. "He's not 'my man,' Granny," I protest weakly.

She winks at me. "Not yet, he isn't. Now get out there and knock his socks off."

Taking a deep breath, I open the door and step out onto the porch. The late afternoon sun warms my skin, and the air is filled with the mouthwatering scents of baked goods and savory treats. I can see Charlie across the street, waving enthusiastically as she arranges plates of cookies on her booth's counter.

And there, walking up the path to my house, is Mark. He's wearing a crisp blue button-down shirt and dark jeans, looking every bit the dashing lawman even in casual clothes. As he gets closer, I notice a bouquet of wildflowers in his hand, and my heart does a little flip.

Granny's ghostly form gives me an enthusiastic spectral thumbs-up, mouthing "Go get 'em, tiger!" Her encouragement, silent though it is, fills me with a surge of confidence.

Mark reaches the bottom of the porch steps, looking up at me with a mixture of admiration and nervousness that mirrors my own feelings. "Lena," he says, his voice warm and slightly husky. "You look... wow."

I feel a blush creeping up my cheeks, but I manage to smile without stammering. "Thanks, Mark. You clean up pretty well yourself."

There's a moment of awkward silence as we both stand there, neither quite sure what to do next. Then, almost in unison, we both start to speak.

"I brought you these—" "Should we get going—"

We stop and laugh, the tension breaking. Mark holds out the flowers. "These are for you. I picked them myself from the meadow just outside town."

As I take the bouquet, our fingers brush, sending a jolt of electricity through me. "They're beautiful," I say softly, inhaling their sweet scent. "Thank you, Mark. That's really thoughtful of you."

He rubs the back of his neck, a gesture I've come to recognize as a sign of his nervousness. "I'm glad you like them. I, uh, I wasn't sure what your favorite flowers were, so I tried to get a variety."

"They're perfect," I assure him, touched by his consideration. "Give me just a second and I'll put them in some water before we go."

When I come back a couple of minutes later, I find Mark watching me with an intensity that makes my pulse quicken.

"Shall we?" he asks, offering me his arm with a charming smile that makes him look boyish and handsome all at once.

I slip my arm through his, feeling myself smiling like a schoolgirl with a crush. "Lead the way, Sheriff."

As we start walking toward the heart of the festival, just steps away from my front yard, I can't help but feel a sense of anticipation. The street is alive with activity—children running between booths, the aroma of freshly baked pies wafting through the air, and the sound of laughter and friendly chatter all around us.

Across the street at her booth, Charlie flashes an exaggerated wink and a thumbs-up that mirror's Granny's. I stifle a laugh, grateful for both of them and their unwavering support. Mark follows my gaze and waves at Charlie, who promptly pretends to be very busy with her cookies.

"So," he says as we stroll past the first few booths, "what would you like to try first? I hear Mrs. Johnson's apple pie is a strong contender for the blue ribbon this year."

I'm about to respond when a commotion further down the street catches our attention. We exchange a glance, both instinctively alert to any sign of trouble. But it's just Mr. Peterson arguing with one of the judges about the proper way to measure flour for a perfect cake.

As the brief excitement dies down, I find myself relaxing into the moment. The warmth of Mark's arm against mine, the festive atmosphere around us, the promise of delicious treats ahead—it all combines to create a sense of contentment I haven't felt in a long time.

"You know what?" I say, smiling up at Mark. "I think I'd like to try everything. We've got all evening, right?"

He grins back at me, his eyes crinkling at the corners in a way that makes my heart skip a beat. “Absolutely. I’m all yours, Lena.”

Chapter 2

The New Oslo Bake-Off is a feast for the senses. As Mark and I stroll down Main Street, arm in arm, I'm overwhelmed by the kaleidoscope of sights, sounds, and smells surrounding us. Colorful booths line both sides of the street, each one a testament to our town's baking prowess. The air is thick with the aroma of cinnamon, vanilla, and freshly baked bread, making my mouth water despite my nervousness.

"Look at all this," I say, gesturing to the bustling scene before us. "I had no idea New Oslo had so many baking enthusiasts."

Mark chuckles, the sound warm and rich. "You'd be surprised. I think half the calls we get at the station are about stolen pie recipes or sabotaged soufflés. And then of course the occasional kitchen fire."

I laugh, relaxing a bit. This is familiar territory—our easy banter about the quirks of small-town life. "Really? And here I thought you spent all your time solving murders with me."

He grins down at me, his eyes twinkling. "Well, that's certainly been the most exciting part of the job lately."

We pass by a booth showcasing an impressive array of elaborately decorated cakes. The baker, Mrs. Thompson, waves at us enthusiastically. "Sheriff! Lena! Come try my red velvet cupcakes!"

Mark looks at me questioningly, and I nod. As we approach the booth, I can't help but admire the intricate sugar flowers adorning each cupcake. Mrs. Thompson beams at us as she hands over two perfect specimens.

"On the house," she says with a wink. "Consider it my contribution to New Oslo's most anticipated first date."

I feel my cheeks flush. "Is everyone in town talking about this?"

Mrs. Thompson laughs. "Honey, when the town's amateur sleuth and the handsome sheriff finally go on a date, it's bigger news than the bake-off itself!"

As we continue our stroll, nibbling on our cupcakes, I can't help but feel a mix of self-consciousness and excitement. The idea that our date is the talk of the town is both flattering and a little overwhelming. I sneak a glance at Mark, wondering if he feels the same way.

He catches me looking and smiles, a bit of frosting on his upper lip. Without thinking, I reach up and wipe it away with my thumb. The moment feels intimate, charged with an electricity that makes my heart race.

"Thanks," he says softly, his eyes never leaving mine.

We're interrupted by a commotion further down the street. A small crowd has gathered around one of the booths, cheering and clapping. Curious, we make our way over.

At the center of the excitement is a woman I recognize as Maggie Fields. She's standing behind a booth laden with pies, her face flushed with joy as she accepts congratulations from the crowd. A large blue ribbon is prominently displayed on the front of her booth.

"Looks like we've found our winner," Mark observes.

As we get closer, Maggie spots us and waves us over eagerly. "Sheriff! Lena! Come taste the pie that won it all!"

We approach the booth, and I'm immediately struck by the mouthwatering aroma of cinnamon and apples. Maggie's eyes are bright with excitement as she cuts us each a slice of her winning pie.

"It's my grandmother's secret recipe," she confides as she hands us our plates. "With a twist, of course. I added a hint of rosemary to the crust. That's what clinched it for the judges, I think."

I take a bite, and the flavors explode on my tongue. The apples are perfectly spiced, the crust flaky and buttery with just a whisper of herbal freshness. "This is amazing, Maggie," I say sincerely. "Congratulations on your win."

Maggie beams at me. "Thank you, Lena! You know, I was so nervous about entering. I almost backed out at the last minute. But my husband insisted, said it was time I showed the world what I could do."

As Maggie chatters on about her baking process, I notice Mark scanning the crowd, his brow furrowed slightly. I follow his gaze and spot a familiar face on the outskirts of the group. Rhonda Peterson is standing apart from the celebratory atmosphere, her arms crossed and her expression distant.

I lean in close to Mark, speaking softly. "Isn't that Rhonda? I thought she was a shoe-in for the blue ribbon this year."

Mark nods, his voice equally low. "She was the runner-up. Apparently, it was a close call between her cherry almond tart and Maggie's apple pie."

I watch as Rhonda's gaze flicks to Maggie, then away again, her jaw tightening. There's something in her expression that tugs at my investigative instincts—a mix of disappointment and... something else. Anger? Resentment?

Before I can ponder it further, I hear a familiar voice calling out to us. "Well, well, well! If it isn't New Oslo's hottest new couple!"

Charlie is weaving through the crowd towards us, her apron now dusted with flour and what looks like chocolate chips. She's grinning from ear to ear as she approaches.

"Charlie!" I exclaim, grateful for the distraction but also a little embarrassed by her enthusiastic greeting. "I thought you were manning your booth?"

She waves a hand dismissively. "I've got my niece covering for me. Couldn't miss the chance to check in on you two lovebirds." She winks at Mark. "So, Sheriff, how are you enjoying your date with our resident mystery solver?"

Mark, to his credit, takes Charlie's teasing in stride. "It's been wonderful so far," he says, smiling at me. "Though I have to say, I didn't expect quite so much... attention around town."

Charlie laughs. "Oh, you should have seen the betting pool at the diner this morning. Half the town was wagering on whether you'd hold hands before or after the pie tasting."

I groan, hiding my face in my hands. "Charlie, please tell me you're joking."

She pats my arm sympathetically. "Don't worry, Lena. I put my money on you two being disgustingly cute the whole time. So far, I'd say I'm winning."

As Charlie continues to regale us with tales of the town's reaction to our date, I find my gaze drawn back to Rhonda. She's moved away from Maggie's booth now, walking with quick, purposeful strides towards the judges' tent. Her posture is rigid, her hands clenched at her sides.

I'm about to mention this to Mark when I catch sight of a familiar spectral form in my peripheral vision. Granny Ingrid is standing – or rather, floating – at the edge of our front yard, just within the boundaries that constrain her ghostly presence. She's waving at me enthusiastically, giving me a thumbs-up and an exaggerated wink.

I can't help but smile at her antics. Even in death, Granny Ingrid is determined to be my personal cheerleader. I give her a subtle wave back, hoping Mark doesn't notice.

"Everything okay?" Mark asks, following my gaze but seeing nothing but the edge of my property.

I nod, turning back to him with a smile. "Everything's perfect," I assure him. And surprisingly, I mean it. Despite the unexpected attention from the people here at the festival and the slight weirdness of having my ghostly grandmother watching from afar, I'm enjoying myself more than I have in a long time.

As Charlie bids us farewell and heads back to her booth, Mark offers me his arm again. "Shall we continue our culinary tour? I heard the main tasting table has all the blue-ribbon winners from the past decade. Might be interesting to compare them to Maggie's pie."

I take his arm, enjoying the warmth of his closeness. "Lead the way, Sheriff. I'm always up for a thorough investigation."

We make our way through the crowd, stopping occasionally to greet neighbors or sample a particularly tempting treat. The festival is in full swing now, with live music playing from a small stage set up in the town square. Couples are dancing, children are running around with faces sticky from cotton candy, and the air is filled with laughter and chatter.

As we approach the main tasting table, I feel a surge of excitement. The crowd here is denser, more focused, everyone eager to sample the best of the best. In the center of the table, displayed on a raised platform, is Maggie's winning apple pie. It's beautifully presented, with delicate lattice work on the crust and a dusting of cinnamon sugar that glitters in the late afternoon sun.

Surrounding Maggie's pie are the blue-ribbon winners from previous years, each looking more delectable than the last. There's a towering chocolate cake with ganache dripping artfully down its sides, a lemon meringue pie with peaks of meringue that seem to defy gravity, and a cheesecake swirled with what looks like homemade raspberry preserves.

"Wow," I breathe, taking in the sight. "I don't know where to start."

Mark grins at me. "Why not start at the beginning? We could work our way through chronologically, ending with Maggie's pie. That way, we can see how the winning recipes have evolved over the years."

I laugh, charmed by his methodical approach. "Always the investigator, aren't you? Alright, let's do it."

We join the line, waiting our turn to taste the blue-ribbon pies and cakes. As we inch closer, I can't help but notice the judges hovering nearby, their expressions a mix of pride and anxiety as they watch people sample the winning entries.

"Nervous bunch, aren't they?" I murmur to Mark.

He nods, his voice low. "Judging the bake-off is a big responsibility in New Oslo. Get it wrong, and you might find yourself persona non grata at the diner for months."

Finally, it's our turn at the table. We start with a slice of pecan pie that won ten years ago, its gooey filling perfectly balanced between sweet and nutty. Next comes a slice of the towering chocolate cake, so rich that a single bite is almost too much. We work our way through each year's winner, trading bites and opinions.

As we near the end of the table, I spot Mr. Fenton, one of the judges, making his way toward us. He's a portly man with a jolly disposition, his round face flushed with excitement.

"Sheriff! Miss Lena!" he calls out. "How are you enjoying our walk through New Oslo's baking history?"

Mark smiles warmly at him. "It's been quite the culinary journey, Mr. Fenton. You and your fellow judges have had your work cut out for you over the years."

Mr. Fenton beams, patting his ample stomach. "It's a tough job, but someone's got to do it. Now, you two simply must try this year's winner. Maggie's pie is something special, let me tell you."

He bustles over to the raised platform where Maggie's apple pie sits in pride of place. With a flourish, he cuts two generous slices and hands them to us on delicate china plates.

"Go on," he urges, watching us expectantly. "Tell me what you think."

I take a bite, closing my eyes to fully appreciate the flavors. The crust is even better than I remember from Maggie's booth—perfectly flaky with that subtle hint of rosemary. The filling is a perfect balance of sweet and tart, the apples maintaining just enough bite to provide a satisfying texture.

"It's wonderful," I say, opening my eyes to see Mr. Fenton nodding in satisfaction.

Mark agrees, his expression one of pleasant surprise. "I'm not usually much for sweets, but this is exceptional. I can see why it won."

Mr. Fenton claps his hands together, looking pleased as punch. "I knew you'd appreciate it. This year's competition was fierce, but Maggie's pie... well, it was a clear winner in the end."

As he speaks, I notice Rhonda Peterson hovering at the edge of the crowd, her eyes fixed on the blue-ribbon pie. There's an intensity to her gaze that makes me uneasy, a hint of something that doesn't quite fit with the festive atmosphere.

Mr. Fenton follows my gaze and his jovial expression falters for a moment. "Ah, yes. Miss Peterson. Her tart was... quite good as well. Very close call, very close indeed."

Before I can ask any questions, Mr. Fenton claps Mark on the shoulder. "Well, I should be making the rounds. Enjoy the rest of the festival, you two. And sheriff," he adds with a wink, "don't let this one get away. She's a keeper!"

As Mr. Fenton wanders off into the crowd, I turn to Mark, ready to share my observations about Rhonda. But the words die on my lips as I see the soft look in his eyes.

"You know," he says, reaching out to tuck a stray lock of hair behind my ear, "as much as I'm enjoying the pie, I think Mr. Fenton might be right about something else entirely."

My heart skips a beat at the warmth in his voice. For a moment, all thoughts of mysterious glances and baking rivalries fade away. In this moment, surrounded by the joy and excitement of the festival, with this handsome man looking at me like that, everything feels perfect.

Chapter 3

The festive atmosphere of the New Oslo Bake-Off shatters in an instant. One moment, Mark and I are standing at the main tasting table, forks poised over slices of Maggie's award-winning apple pie. The next, a collective gasp ripples through the crowd, followed by a sickening thud.

I turn just in time to see Arnold McCarthy, the head judge, crumple to the ground like a marionette with its strings cut. For a heartbeat, everything seems to freeze—the cheerful chatter, the music from the nearby bandstand, even the warm early evening breeze. Then, chaos erupts.

"Arnold!" someone screams, the sound piercing through the sudden shocked silence. It's as if that single cry opens the floodgates, and suddenly the air is filled with shouts, screams, and a rising tide of panic.

Mark reacts instantly, his sheriff's instincts kicking in. He's already moving toward Arnold before I can even process what's happening. "Everyone, stay back!" he shouts, his voice cutting through the noise. "Give him some space!"

I watch as Mark kneels beside Arnold's prone form, rolling him onto his side as his fingers search for a pulse at his neck. Even from where I stand, I can see the growing pallor of Arnold's skin, the unnatural stillness of his chest.

"Someone call 911!" Mark yells. "We need medical assistance now!"

My own heart is racing, adrenaline surging through my veins. I want to help, but I know the best thing I can do right now is stay out of the way.

That's when I see it—a flash of metal protruding from Arnold's chest, barely visible from where I'm standing and completely hidden from Mark's point of view. My breath catches in my throat as I realize what I'm looking at: the handle of a paring knife, buried to the hilt in Arnold's heart.

"Mark," I call out, working my way closer so I don't have to shout the alarming news as loudly. "Mark, it's not a heart attack. He's been stabbed."

Mark's head snaps up, his eyes meeting mine for a brief, intense moment. I see the shift in his expression as he processes my words and then spots the knife. In that instant, I watch the last remnants of my perfect date disappear completely.

"Everyone, step back!" Mark orders, his voice ringing with authority. "This is now a crime scene. Nobody leaves the area!"

The crowd, already agitated, becomes even more frenzied at this announcement. I hear murmurs of disbelief, see faces contort with shock and fear. A few people try to push their way out of the cordoned-off area, but Mark's deputies, who seemed to materialize out of nowhere, quickly intercept them.

"Lena," Mark says, catching my attention. His face is grim, all traces of our earlier lightheartedness gone. "I need you to stay here, okay? Don't touch anything, don't go anywhere. I know you want to help, but right now, the best thing you can do is be a witness."

"Of course," I nod, though I feel like there's a bit of an unspoken message as well. Surely he wants me to observe, to use my keen eye for detail to take in everything around us. Even as he speaks, I'm already cataloging the scene—the position of Arnold's body, the faces in the crowd, the layout of the tasting table.

As Mark turns away to coordinate with his deputies, I notice movement near the edge of the crowd. Maggie Fields, the triumphant winner of the bake-off, is pushing her way forward, her face a mask of horror.

"No, no, no," she's muttering, her eyes fixed on Arnold's motionless form. "This can't be happening. Not now, not like this."

She reaches the police tape that's being hastily strung up around the scene, her hands clutching at it as if it's the only thing keeping her upright. "My pie," she says, her voice rising hysterically. "It wasn't my pie, was it? Oh god, did someone poison my pie?"

A deputy gently but firmly pushes her back, but Maggie seems beyond reason. "You don't understand!" she cries out. "I won fair and square! My pie had nothing to do with this! Nothing!"

Her outburst draws attention, and I see heads turning, whispers spreading through the crowd like wildfire. The joyous celebration of just minutes ago has transformed into a roiling sea of suspicion and fear.

As I watch Maggie's breakdown, movement in my peripheral vision catches my eye. Rhonda Peterson, the runner-up whose tense behavior I'd noticed earlier, is slowly backing away from the scene. Her face is a study in conflicting emotions—shock, certainly, but also something else. Relief? Guilt? It's gone too quickly for me to be sure, hidden behind a mask of appropriate horror as she melts into the background of the milling crowd.

I make a mental note to mention Rhonda's behavior to Mark later. Right now, he's too busy coordinating the initial investigation, calling in additional officers and trying to maintain some semblance of order in the chaos.

As I continue to observe, I can't help but notice the faces of other bakers and contestants. Some are openly weeping, others stand in stunned silence. A few are huddled together, whispering frantically. I wonder how many of them had interacted with Arnold today, how many might have had a reason to want him out of the way.

The sound of approaching sirens cuts through the air, growing louder by the second. Soon, the area is flooded with paramedics and additional police officers. I watch as they swarm around Arnold's body, their movements efficient but ultimately futile. I already know what their verdict will be.

After what seems like hours but is probably only minutes, Mark makes his way back to me. His face is drawn, his earlier warmth replaced by the cool professionalism of a lawman with a job to do.

"Lena," he sighs, his voice low and tinged with regret. "I'm sorry, but I think it's pretty clear our date is over."

I nod, feeling a pang of disappointment in spite of the gravity of the situation. "I understand, Mark. You have a job to do."

He runs a hand through his hair, a gesture of frustration that I've come to recognize. "This is bad, Lena. Really bad. A murder, right here in the middle of the bake-off? The whole town is going to be in an uproar."

"I know," I say softly. "But if anyone can handle it, you can."

He gives me a wan smile. "Thanks for the vote of confidence. Look, I hate to ask this of you, but..."

"You want me to stay out of it," I finish for him, already knowing where this is going.

Mark sighs. "I know it's a lot to ask, given your... history with these kinds of cases. But this is different, Lena. You're a witness this time. If we hadn't been standing next to each other, I'd say maybe even a potential suspect given how close we were to the scene."

I raise an eyebrow at that. "A suspect? Really, Mark? That would make you a suspect, too, wouldn't it?"

He holds up his hands placatingly. "I know you didn't do this, Lena. I'll only be questioning you as a witness. I'm just saying that my job requires me to consider every possibility. It's nothing personal, you know that. Just... promise me you'll let me handle this one, okay?"

I nod, but even as I do, I know it's a promise I'm unlikely to keep. It's not that I don't trust Mark—I do, implicitly. But I also know that my unique perspective, my ability to see connections that others might miss, could be crucial in solving this case.

As Mark turns away to continue coordinating the investigation, I cast my gaze once more over the scene. The bright, cheerful decorations of the bake-off now seem garish and out of place against the backdrop of flashing police lights.

In the span of mere minutes, our perfect first date has transformed into a nightmare. But as I watch Mark move through the crowd, calm and competent, I feel a surge of determination. This may not be how I envisioned our evening ending, but one thing is certain—I'm going to get to the bottom of this mystery, with or without Mark's blessing.

Chapter 4

I watch from the sidelines as Mark efficiently coordinates his deputies, cordoning off the area and beginning to question the shell-shocked festival attendees. His face is a mask of professional determination, but I can see the tension in the set of his shoulders, the furrow of his brow.

He told me to let him take the lead on this one, and I certainly don't want to do anything that might interfere with his investigation. But that doesn't mean I have to sit on my hands the whole time.

I just have to be mindful not to cross any lines—either professionally or personally.

Besides, my mind is already whirling with theories and possibilities that will require some peace and quiet and my own familiar space to sort out.

As I approach my front yard, I spot Granny Ingrid's ghostly form pacing—or rather, floating back and forth—at the edge of the property. Her spectral face is creased with worry, and she rushes towards me as soon as I'm within earshot.

"Lena! What in tarnation is going on out there? I saw the ambulance and all those police cars. Don't tell me someone's gone and ruined your date by dying!"

I can't help but let out a wry chuckle at her blunt assessment. "I'm afraid so, Granny. Arnold McCarthy, the head judge, was murdered right in front of the main tasting table."

Granny Ingrid's eyes widen, her transparent form flickering with shock. "Murdered? Arnold? Well, I'll be... Who'd want to kill that old coot?"

I shake my head, sinking down onto the porch steps. "That's the million-dollar question, isn't it? And one I intend to figure out."

Granny settles beside me, or as close to beside me as her ghostly constraints will allow. "Well then, let's get to it. You know I hear all sorts of things from folks passing by. Between your detecting skills and my gossip network, we'll crack this case in no time."

For the next hour, Granny and I pool our knowledge, piecing together a list of potential suspects. By the time we're done, four names stand out:

There's Maggie Fields, the beaming winner whose triumph has been tainted by tragedy. Then of course Rhonda Peterson, the runner-up whose odd behavior caught my eye even before the murder.

There were also a couple of other names and faces I wasn't familiar with, but who Granny assured me might have a metaphorical—or literal—ax to grind with poor Arnold. For starters, there's Grant McCarthy, Arnold's estranged son who, according to Granny, has a rocky history with his father. Then there's Betty O'Connor, a long-time rival of Maggie's in both baking and local politics.

The four of them seem as good a place as any to start asking questions and trying to piece together what might have happened in the time leading up to Arnold's murder.

"And don't forget," Granny adds, wagging a spectral finger at me, "Betty's been trying to get on the judging panel for years. Always said Arnold was biased against her."

I'm about to respond when I spot Charlie making her way up the path, her earlier cheerfulness replaced by a worried frown.

"Lena!" she calls out as she approaches. "Are you okay? I saw what happened and I've been trying to get over here, but they wouldn't let anyone leave their booths for ages."

I stand to meet her, grateful for her concern. "I'm fine, Charlie. Just trying to make sense of it all."

Charlie glances at the spot where Granny Ingrid is hovering, clearly seeing nothing but empty air. "Were you talking to yourself or to Granny Ingrid when I walked up just now?"

I share a quick, amused look with Granny before turning back to Charlie. "A little of both, if I'm being honest. Come on, I'll fill you in on what I know so far."

As we settle onto the porch swing, I run through the events of the afternoon and the list of suspects Granny and I have compiled. Charlie listens intently, her eyes widening as I detail my observations.

"Wow," she breathes when I finish. "I can't believe this is happening. Poor Arnold... and on your first date with Mark, too!"

I nod, feeling a pang of disappointment at the reminder of our interrupted evening. "I know. It's an awful situation all around."

Charlie's expression turns serious. "Lena, you're not thinking of investigating this yourself, are you? I mean, I know it's kind of your thing, but Mark specifically asked you to stay out of it, right?"

I sigh, avoiding her gaze. "I know he did, but Charlie, you know I can help. I see things others might miss."

"I get it. I do," Charlie says, placing a hand on my arm. "But please be careful, okay? This isn't like your other cases. You were right there when it happened. You could be in danger."

Her words send a chill down my spine, but they also strengthen my resolve. "All the more reason to figure out who did this," I say firmly.

Charlie shakes her head, a mix of exasperation and fondness in her expression. "I know that look. Just... promise me you'll be careful?"

I nod, giving her hand a squeeze. "I promise. Now, I think it's time I did some investigating of my own."

Leaving Charlie to head back to her booth, I make my way towards the festival grounds. The police have started allowing some of the vendors to return to their stations, though the area around the main tasting table remains blocked off.

I spot Maggie Fields at her booth, her earlier jubilation replaced by a haunted look. As I approach, she glances up, her eyes red-rimmed and fearful.

"Lena," she says, her voice trembling. "Is he really dead? I saw him lying there. I saw the blood. I just... I keep hoping for a miracle, or that my eyes were playing tricks on me."

I nod solemnly. "I'm afraid it's true, Maggie. I'm so sorry. I know how upsetting this must be."

Maggie's face crumples, fresh tears spilling down her cheeks. "I just can't believe it. One minute I'm on top of the world, and the next..." She trails off, shaking her head. "People are going to blame me, aren't they? Because I won. They'll think I had something to do with it."

I lean in, keeping my voice low and reassuring. "Maggie, no one's blaming you. Can you think of anyone who might have wanted to harm Arnold? Did you notice anything unusual before it happened?"

She shakes her head, wiping at her eyes. "No, nothing. Everything seemed normal. Well, except..."

"Except what?" I prompt gently.

Maggie hesitates, then leans in closer. "Well, I did overhear Arnold arguing with someone earlier. I couldn't see who it was, but he seemed really upset. Said something about 'coming clean' and 'making things right.' I didn't think much of it at the time, but now..."

I nod, filing this information away. "Thank you, Maggie. That could be important."

As I turn to leave, my eye catches on a figure lurking across the street from where we are. Rhonda Peterson is standing half-hidden behind a tree, her posture tense and wary. When she notices me looking her way, she quickly turns and disappears into the dispersing crowd.

Frowning, I make a mental note to try and find Rhonda later. Her behavior is becoming increasingly suspicious.

As I continue my rounds, I overhear snippets of conversation from the milling crowd. One exchange, in particular, catches my attention.

"Did you see Grant McCarthy?" an older woman is saying to her companion. "Arnold's son? He showed up late to the Bake-Off, barely said two words to his father before... well, you know."

Her friend nods sagely. "I heard they've been on the outs for years. Something about Grant feeling like his father never supported his dreams of becoming a chef."

I file this information away, my mind racing. Seems like Granny's hunch might have been right about Grant, the estranged son with a potential grudge.

As the afternoon wears on, I can feel the weight of the day's events settling over me. What started as a promising first date has turned into a nightmare of suspicion and fear. The cheerful decorations of the Bake-Off now seem almost mocking, a stark contrast to the somber mood that has descended on New Oslo.

I catch sight of Mark in the distance, deep in conversation with one of his deputies. Our eyes meet for a brief moment, and I see a mix of emotions flash across his face—concern, frustration, and something softer that makes my heart skip a beat.

I know he wants me to stay out of this, to let him handle the investigation. But as I look around at the familiar faces of my neighbors, now clouded with fear and suspicion, I know I can't just stand by. New Oslo is my home now, and someone has shattered the peace of our little community.

With renewed determination, I straighten my shoulders and head back towards my house. I have a murder to solve, a killer to catch, and a date to reschedule.

Chapter 5

When it's all over and the crowds have mostly dispersed, I'm walking back home when I spot Mark making his way toward me, his broad shoulders slightly hunched with the weight of the day's events.

"Lena," he says softly as he reaches me. His eyes are clouded with fatigue and concern. "I'm so sorry about all of this. Not exactly the first date I had in mind."

I manage a small smile, trying to lighten the mood. "Well, you certainly know how to show a girl an exciting time, Sheriff."

He chuckles, but it's a hollow sound. He runs a hand through his sandy hair, mussing it up in a way that I find endearing despite the circumstances. "Can we talk privately for a moment?" he asks, gesturing towards a quiet corner away from the crime scene.

When we're out of earshot of the remaining officers and passers-by, Mark turns to face me, his expression serious. "Lena, I know you. I know that curious mind of yours is already working overtime on this case." He pauses, seeming to choose his next words carefully. "I need to ask you, as both the sheriff and... well, as someone who cares about you, to please stay out of this investigation."

I feel a familiar spark of defiance ignite within me. I open my mouth to protest, but Mark holds up a hand, his eyes pleading.

"I know it's a lot to ask," he continues. "But this is a delicate situation. Arnold was a prominent member of the community, and his death is going to have far-reaching consequences. We need to handle this by the book."

I bite my lip, weighing my words. I know I can't make a promise I have no intention of keeping. "I understand, Mark," I say finally, my voice deliberately vague. "I'll do my best to stay out of your way."

Mark's shoulders relax slightly, but there's a flicker of doubt in his eyes. He knows me too well to be completely reassured by my non-committal response. "Thank you, Lena. I appreciate that."

As we stand there, the tension of the day's events hanging between us, I find myself acutely aware of my growing attraction to Mark. It isn't just his rugged good looks or his kind heart—it's the way he respects my intelligence, even as he tries to protect me. But with that attraction comes a new set of complications.

My mind races, considering the potential fallout of my inevitable involvement in the case. Will my sleuthing drive a wedge between us before our relationship even has a chance to begin? Or will Mark come to appreciate my investigative skills, seeing them as a complement to his own?

The uncertainty gnaws at me, but the pull of the mystery is too strong to ignore. I know, deep down, that I will find a way to unravel this puzzle, with or without Mark's approval.

As if sensing my internal struggle, Mark's expression softens. "I know this isn't easy for you," he says gently. "Your curiosity and your desire to help are part of what makes you... well, you." He pauses, a hint of a smile playing at the corners of his mouth. "It's part of what drew me to you in the first place."

I smile. He does know me pretty well. Maybe a little too well, sometimes. "Mark, I—"

But before I can finish, Mark's radio crackles to life, demanding his attention. He gives me an apologetic look as he answers the call, stepping away slightly to speak in hushed tones with one of his deputies.

I watch him, my mind whirring with possibilities based on what I already know about the case. I know I should respect his wishes and stay out of the investigation, but the temptation to dig deeper is almost overwhelming. Maybe if I can just get a little more information, I can satisfy my curiosity and turn it all over to him without fully involving myself.

As Mark finishes his call and turns back to me, I make a split-second decision. "Mark," I say, my voice taking on a casual tone that I hope masks my eagerness, "I know you can't share details of the investigation, but... is there anything you can tell me? Anything at all that might help me understand what happened?"

Mark hesitates, clearly torn between his professional duties and his desire to confide in me. After a moment, he sighs. "I probably shouldn't say anything, but..." He glances around, ensuring we're still alone. "Arnold mentioned something to one of the other judges just before the festival started. Said he was planning to 'come clean' about some secret."

My eyebrows shoot up. That sounds a lot like the tidbit of information I heard from Maggie. "A secret? Did he say what kind of secret?"

Mark shakes his head. "No details, I'm afraid. But it could be connected to the motive. We're looking into his personal and professional life, trying to figure out what he might have been referring to."

A secret significant enough to prompt a confession, and potentially significant enough to lead to murder? I try to keep my expression neutral, not wanting to betray my intense interest. "That's... intriguing," I say carefully.

Encouraged by Mark's willingness to share, I decide to press my luck a little further. "What about the murder weapon? Have you been able to trace it?"

Mark runs a hand over his face, looking torn. Finally, he seems to come to a decision. "Okay, but this stays between us, right?" At my eager nod, he continues, "The knife used in the stabbing... it belonged to one of the baking booths. We're still trying to determine exactly which one, but it narrows down our list of suspects considerably."

My heart races at this new information. The murder weapon coming from one of the booths suggests that the killer is likely someone involved in the Bake-Off, either as a contestant or perhaps as staff. My mind immediately flies to the suspects Granny Ingrid and I had discussed: Maggie Fields, Rhonda Peterson, and Betty O'Connor. Any one of them could have had access to a knife from one of the booths. Even Grant, Arnold's estranged son, could've picked up an unattended knife easily enough.

But then, so could anyone else.

"Thank you for telling me, Mark," I say softly, genuinely appreciative of his trust in me. "I know it's not easy for you to share details of the case."

Mark nods, his expression a mix of affection and concern. "I just hope it helps put your mind at ease a bit. Maybe satisfies that curiosity of yours enough to keep you from... well, you know."

I give him a small smile, guilt tugging at my conscience. In spite of his hopes, this information has only fueled my desire to investigate further. But I push that thought aside for now, focusing instead on the man standing in front of me.

"Listen, Lena," Mark says, his voice taking on a softer tone. "I know this isn't how either of us envisioned our first date going. But I was wondering... maybe we could try again? Once things settle down a bit, of course."

I feel a flutter of excitement in my stomach. Despite the grim circumstances surrounding us, the prospect of a proper date with Mark is too good to pass up. "I'd like that," I reply, my smile genuine this time.

Mark's face lights up with relief and happiness. "Great! I promise, no murder investigations next time. Just you, me, and a nice, quiet evening."

But even as I bask in the glow of our rescheduled date, a part of my mind is already turning over the new information I've learned. The secret Arnold had planned to reveal, the murder weapon from one of the booths—these are crucial pieces of the puzzle I'm determined to solve.

As if sensing my distraction, Mark squeezes my hand gently. "I should get back to work," he says reluctantly. "But I'll call you soon about that date, okay?"

I nod, watching as Mark makes his way back to the crime scene. I stand there for a moment longer, caught between two powerful forces: my growing feelings for Mark and my insatiable curiosity about the murder I've witnessed with my own two eyes.

As I finally turn to head home, my mind is a whirlwind of conflicting emotions. Excitement about my future with Mark wars with frustration at having to keep my inevitable investigation a secret from him. The thrill of new information battles with the weight of the promise I've made to stay out of the case.

But underneath it all, there's a sense of determination. I know that, one way or another, I will uncover the truth behind Arnold McCarthy's murder. I just hope that in doing so, I won't jeopardize the budding relationship that holds so much promise.

As I walk through the quiet streets of New Oslo, the cool night air clearing my head, I begin to formulate a plan. I'll need to be careful, to investigate discreetly without arousing Mark's suspicions. It will be a delicate balance, but I'm confident in my abilities.

After all, I've solved mysteries before, and I have a secret weapon that the police don't have—the ghostly assistance of Granny Ingrid. With her spectral insights and my own sharp mind, we stand a good chance of cracking the case.

As I approach my home, I can almost hear Granny Ingrid's excited voice, eager to hear about the new developments. I smile to myself, knowing that a long night of theorizing and planning lies ahead.

Chapter 6

It's a clear, bright blue morning, but there's a weight on my shoulders that's keeping me from enjoying the near-perfect weather. I'm headed to Maggie Fields' house, and my heart is pounding with a mix of anticipation and nervousness. As the winner of the ill-fated Bake-Off, Maggie is at the center of this mystery, whether she knows it or not.

I rehearse my approach in my head as I walk. I'm not here to accuse or interrogate, I remind myself. I'm just a concerned friend, checking in after a traumatic event. But beneath that facade, my mind is sharp, ready to catch any detail that might shed light on Arnold's murder.

Maggie's house comes into view—a charming Victorian with gingerbread trim and a wraparound porch. Similar to my Granny's house, in fact, aside from the not-so-cheerful vibes I get as I walk up to the door. The garden, usually immaculate, shows signs of neglect. A few weeds have sprung up among the mums, and fallen leaves litter the path. It's a small detail, but it speaks volumes about Maggie's state of mind.

I take a deep breath and knock on the door. For a moment, there's silence, and I wonder if she's even home. Then I hear shuffling footsteps, and the door creaks open.

It's hard to suppress a gasp at the sight when Maggie peers out from her darkened foyer. The perfectly coiffed, eternally cheerful woman I know has been replaced by someone I barely recognize. Her hair is disheveled, dark circles ring her eyes, and she's still wearing what looks like yesterday's clothes and makeup.

"Lena," she frowns, her voice hoarse. "What are you doing here?"

I paste on my most sympathetic smile. "I came to check on you, Maggie. After what happened yesterday... well, I thought you might need a friend."

For a moment, Maggie looks like she might close the door in my face. Then her shoulders slump, and she steps back. "Come on in."

I follow her into the living room, my eyes darting around, taking in every detail. The usually spotless house is in disarray—dishes are piled in the sink, a half-empty glass of wine is sitting on the coffee table, baking supplies are scattered across the kitchen counter. The whole place is disheveled and dark, and I'm actually a little concerned for Maggie's state of mind right now.

She sinks into an armchair, and I perch on the edge of the sofa across from her. "How are you holding up?" I ask gently.

Maggie lets out a bitter laugh. "How do you think? I finally win the blue ribbon, and instead of celebrating, I'm wondering if I'm going to be arrested for murder."

I lean forward, keeping my voice soft and non-threatening. "Maggie, no one thinks you killed Arnold. You were up on stage when it happened, remember?"

She nods, but I can see the fear hasn't left her eyes. "I know, but... people will talk. They'll wonder. Maybe they'll think I had something to do with it, even if I didn't... didn't do it myself."

I watch her carefully, noting the way her hands tremble, the sheen of sweat on her forehead. She's clearly shaken, but is it just from the shock of the murder, or is there something more?

"Can you tell me about yesterday?" I ask. "Before... well, before it happened. How did you feel about the competition?"

Her eyes light up for a moment, a ghost of her usual enthusiasm shining through. "I was so excited. I've been entering the contest for years, you know. Never even placed before. But this year, I was determined. I practiced that apple pie recipe for months, perfecting every detail."

As she speaks, I can hear the passion in her voice. This wasn't just a hobby for Maggie—it was an obsession. "It must have been a lot of work," I prompt.

She nods vigorously. "Oh, it was. I tried every type of apple, every variation of crust. I even ordered special pie tins from Europe that supposedly hold just the right amount of filling to keep a perfect ratio with the crust." She pauses, a shadow passing over her face. "I... I worked so hard. I deserved to win. I did win."

There's something in her tone, a desperate edge that makes me wonder. How far would Maggie go to ensure her victory? I push the thought aside for now, focusing on keeping her talking.

"And the judging?" I ask casually. "How did that go?"

Maggie's expression becomes guarded. "It was... fair enough, I suppose. Arnold always tried to be impartial."

I raise an eyebrow at her choice of words. "Fair enough? That sounds like you might have had some doubts."

She shifts uncomfortably in her seat. "No, no, nothing like that. Arnold was... he was a good judge. It's just..." She trails off, biting her lip.

I lean in, my curiosity piqued. "It's just what, Maggie?"

But she shakes her head, forcing a smile that doesn't reach her eyes. "Nothing. I'm just tired and upset. This whole situation is so awful."

I nod sympathetically, but my mind is racing. What was Maggie about to say? What doubts did she have about Arnold's judging?

Before I can probe further, there's a sharp knock at the door. Maggie jumps, her eyes wide with fear. "Who could that be?" she whispers.

"Do you want me to get it?" I offer, but she's already standing, smoothing her rumpled clothes.

"No, no, I've got it," she says, hurrying to the door.

I hear muffled voices, then Maggie returns, looking flustered. "It's Betty O'Connor," she says. "She wants to talk to me about... about yesterday. Would you mind...?"

"Of course," I say, standing up. "I'll just step out onto the porch for a moment. Get some fresh air."

Maggie nods gratefully, and I make my way outside. But instead of descending the steps, I linger near the partly open window, my conscience wrestling with my curiosity. This isn't right, I tell myself, even as I'm literally eavesdropping. But if Betty has information about the murder...

I lean closer to the window, straining to hear.

"...can't believe you have the nerve to show your face," Betty's voice hisses. "After what you did."

"I don't know what you're talking about," Maggie replies, her voice trembling.

"Oh, please," Betty scoffs. "You expect me to believe you won that ribbon fair and square? After years of mediocre pies, suddenly you're a baking genius? What did you do, Maggie? Bribe the judges? Cheat?"

My eyes widen at Betty's accusation. Could it be true? Had Maggie really cheated her way to victory?

"That's ridiculous," Maggie protests, but there's a note of panic in her voice. "I worked hard for that win. I deserved it!"

"Did Arnold think so, too?" Betty's voice drips with venom. "Is that why he's dead? Because he found out what you did?"

There's a crash—the sound of breaking glass—and I have to resist the urge to run back inside.

"Get out," Maggie says, her voice low and dangerous. "Get out of my house right now."

I hear the sound of retreating footsteps, then the slam of the front door. Taking a deep breath, I count to ten before re-entering the house.

Maggie is standing in the middle of the living room, a broken wine glass at her feet. She looks up as I enter, her face a mask of misery.

"Maggie?" I say softly. "Are you okay? I heard raised voices."

She shakes her head, bending down to pick up the broken glass. "It's nothing. Betty's just... she's always been jealous of anyone who does well in the Bake-Off. Especially now that the person happens to be me."

I kneel down to help her, watching her face carefully. "She seemed pretty upset. Was it about the competition?"

Maggie's hand trembles, and a piece of glass slips, nicking her finger. She hisses in pain, a drop of blood welling up. "It's stupid," she mutters. "She thinks... she thinks I must have cheated somehow. As if I'd ever do something like that."

I hand her a tissue for her cut, my mind whirling. Betty's accusation, Maggie's reaction—there's more going on here than just sour grapes over a baking competition.

"Maggie," I say carefully, "I know this is a difficult time, but... is there anything you want to tell me? About the competition, or Arnold, or anything?"

For a moment, I think she might confide in me. There's a look in her eyes, a mixture of fear and desperation that makes my heart ache. But then she shakes her head, the moment passing.

"There's nothing to tell," she says firmly. "I won fair and square. Arnold was a good judge. What happened to him is terrible, but it has nothing to do with me or the Bake-Off."

I nod, not pushing further. But as I help her clean up the rest of the broken glass, I can't shake the feeling that Maggie is hiding something. The question is, what? And how is it connected to Arnold's murder?

As we finish cleaning, I notice Maggie glancing nervously toward the kitchen. Following her gaze, I spot a cabinet door slightly ajar. "Everything okay?" I ask casually.

Maggie startles, quickly moving to close the cabinet. "Oh, yes, just... just some baking supplies I need to put away."

But in that brief moment before the door closes, I catch a glimpse of something inside. Ribbons – dozens of them, in various colors. Far more than I've ever seen Maggie win at the local competitions.

My mind races with questions. Where did all those ribbons come from? And why is Maggie hiding them?

I force a smile, pretending I haven't noticed anything unusual. "Well, I should probably get going. Thanks for talking to me, Maggie. And remember, if you need anything, I'm just a phone call away. Seriously. Anything at all."

I mean that last part genuinely. Even though I'm curious about her possible motives, I'm more concerned that she's spiraling without anyone else to talk to.

She nods distractedly, walking me to the door. As I step out onto the porch, I turn back to her. "Oh, by the way, have you heard from Rhonda since yesterday? I was thinking of checking in on her too."

Maggie's reaction is subtle, but unmistakable. Her body tenses, her eyes widening slightly before she controls her expression. "Rhonda? No, I... I haven't spoken to her. Why do you ask?"

I shrug, keeping my tone casual. "No reason. Just thought I'd check on everyone involved in the Bake-Off. This must be hard on all of you."

Maggie nods stiffly. "Yes, well, I'm sure Rhonda's fine. She... she's tough, you know."

As I walk away from Maggie's house, my mind is buzzing with new information and even more questions. Maggie's nervous behavior, Betty's accusations, the hidden stash of ribbons, and that strange reaction to Rhonda's name—it all adds up to something.

But does it add up to murder?

Chapter 7

The warm, comforting scent of freshly baked bread and cinnamon embraces me as I step into Sweet Surprises, Rhonda Peterson's bakery. It's early afternoon, typically a busy time for the shop, but today the tables are empty, and there's no line at the counter.

Rhonda is behind the display case, mechanically arranging a tray of scones. She looks up at the sound of the door, and I can see the toll the past day has taken on her. Her usually bright eyes are dull and rimmed with red, and there's a slight tremor in her hands as she sets down the tray.

"Lena," she says, her voice hoarse. "I... I wasn't expecting to see you here."

I approach the counter, trying to keep my posture open and non-threatening. "Hi, Rhonda. I just wanted to check in on you. After everything that happened yesterday..."

Rhonda's shoulders slump, and for a moment, I think she might break down right here and now. But she takes a deep breath, squaring her shoulders. "It's been... difficult," she admits. "I still can't believe Arnold is gone. It doesn't seem real."

I nod sympathetically, watching her closely. "I can't imagine how you must be feeling. You and Arnold worked closely together on the bake-off committee, didn't you?"

A flicker of something—fear? guilt?—passes across Rhonda's face before she schools her expression. "Yes, we did. Arnold was... he was a good man. A fair judge."

There's a catch in her voice on the word "fair" that piques my interest. "It must be hard," I say gently, "coming so close to winning and then... this."

Rhonda's head snaps up, her eyes flashing. "Is that what you think this is about? That I'm upset about losing? That I would... that I could..." She breaks off, her voice choked with emotion.

I hold up my hands placatingly. "No, no, of course not. I'm sorry, Rhonda. I didn't mean to imply anything. I know you'd never hurt Arnold."

She nods, but I can see she's still on edge. I decide to change tack, remembering what Mark had told me about Arnold's cryptic comments before the festival.

"Rhonda," I say carefully, "I heard that Arnold was acting a bit... distracted during the judging. That he mentioned something about 'coming clean.' Did he say anything to you about that?"

The effect of my words is immediate and startling. Rhonda goes pale, her hands gripping the edge of the counter so tightly her knuckles turn white. "Who told you that?" she demands, her voice barely above a whisper.

I keep my tone casual, even as my heart races with the knowledge that I've struck a nerve. "Oh, you know how people talk in a small town. I just wondered if you'd noticed anything."

Rhonda's eyes dart around the empty bakery as if checking for eavesdroppers. When she speaks, her voice is low and strained. "I don't know anything about that. Arnold was... he was focused on the judging. That's all."

But I can see the lie in her eyes, in the way she won't quite meet my gaze. There's something more here, something that has

Rhonda terrified. And I'm beginning to suspect it has little to do with the bake-off itself.

I lean in, lowering my voice conspiratorially. "Rhonda, if there's something you know, something that might help figure out what happened to Arnold, you should tell the police. No one would blame you for—"

"No!" The force of Rhonda's exclamation startles us both. She takes a shaky breath, visibly trying to calm herself. "I mean, there's nothing to tell. Nothing that would help, anyway."

I watch her carefully, noting the way her eyes keep darting to the clock on the wall, the nervous energy thrumming through her body. It's clear she's worried about something, but it doesn't seem to be related to the contest or even directly to Arnold's murder.

A suspicion begins to form in my mind, one that makes my stomach churn uncomfortably. Could Rhonda and Arnold have been... involved? The thought of the kindly judge in a secret affair seems absurd, but it would explain Rhonda's extreme distress and her reluctance to talk.

I decide to probe a little further, treading carefully. "Rhonda," I begin, keeping my voice gentle, "I know Arnold was more than just a judge to you. You worked closely together for years. If there was... anything else between you, anything you're worried about people finding out—"

"It wasn't like that!" Rhonda interrupts, her cheeks flushing. "Arnold and I were friends, colleagues. Nothing more."

I nod, but I can see my words have struck a chord. Rhonda is fiddling with her apron, her eyes downcast. "I'm sorry," I say softly. "I didn't mean to upset you. I just want to understand what happened."

Rhonda is silent for a long moment, and I can almost see the internal struggle playing out on her face. When she finally speaks, her voice is so quiet I have to lean in to hear her.

"Arnold was... he was planning to reveal something. Before the end of the festival."

My heart leaps at this confirmation of what Mark had told me. "Reveal what?" I ask, trying to keep the eagerness out of my voice.

Rhonda shakes her head, looking miserable. "I don't know exactly. He didn't tell me the details. But he said... he said it would change everything."

I feel a rush of excitement mixed with dread. What could Arnold have known that was so important? And could it have been the reason for his murder?

"Rhonda," I say urgently, "this is important. If Arnold was planning to reveal something, it could be connected to what happened to him. You need to tell the police—"

But my words seem to snap Rhonda out of her momentary openness. Her face closes off, and she straightens up, stepping back from the counter. "No," she says firmly. "I've already said too much. This... this isn't any of your business, Lena. Please, just leave it alone."

I open my mouth to protest, but the look in Rhonda's eyes stops me. There's fear there, yes, but also a steely determination. I realize that pushing her further right now will only make her clam up completely.

"Okay," I say, holding up my hands in surrender. "I'm sorry for prying. I just... I care about this town, and about you. I want to help."

Rhonda's expression softens slightly. "I know you do, Lena. But trust me, the best thing you can do right now is to let the police handle this. Please."

I nod, knowing that for now, at least, I've gotten all I can from Rhonda. "Okay. But if you need anything, or if you change your mind about talking, you know where to find me."

As I turn to leave, Rhonda calls out, her voice trembling slightly. "Lena? Be careful. There's... there's more going on here than you know."

I look back at her, taking in the fear in her eyes, the tension in her posture. "I will," I promise. "You be careful too, Rhonda."

I step out onto the street, my mind whirling with everything I've learned—and everything I still don't know.

One thing is clear: Rhonda knows something crucial about Arnold's murder. Her reaction to my questions, her slip about Arnold's planned revelation—it all adds up to a secret that's eating her alive. But what could it be? And how far would she go to protect it?

As I walk home, my steps quick with nervous energy, I run through the possibilities. An affair seems the most likely explanation, but something about that doesn't sit right with me. Arnold had always seemed so devoted to his wife, and Rhonda's reaction didn't quite fit with a guilty lover.

No, there's something else going on here. Something big enough to change everything, as Rhonda had said. Something that multiple people—Rhonda, Maggie, maybe even Betty—seem to be tangled up in.

I think back to the hidden ribbons in Maggie's kitchen, to Betty's furious accusations of cheating. Could Arnold have uncovered some kind of long-running scam in the baking competition circuit? It seems absurd—who would kill over a blue ribbon?—but in a small town like New Oslo, reputations and livelihoods can hinge on the smallest things.

Or perhaps it's something bigger, something that goes beyond our little town. Arnold had been a judge in state and even national competitions. Could he have stumbled upon something more sinister in the wider world of competitive baking?

As I reach my front porch, I'm more convinced than ever that Rhonda's secret is the key to this whole case. But how can I uncover it without putting her—or myself—in danger?

Chapter 8

I close the door behind me, leaning against it with a heavy sigh. The weight of everything I've learned today settles on my shoulders like a physical burden. Rhonda's secret, Maggie's hidden ribbons, Betty's accusations—it all swirls in my mind, a jumble of clues that I can't quite piece together.

"Well, you certainly look like you've had quite a day."

I start at the sound of Granny Ingrid's voice, my heart racing. Even after all this time, I'm still not totally used to her ghostly appearances. She's sitting—or rather, floating—in her favorite armchair, her spectral form shimmering slightly in the afternoon light.

"Granny," I exhale, relief washing over me. If anyone can help me make sense of this mess, it's her. "I'm so glad you're here. I don't know what to make of everything I've learned."

Her eyes twinkle with that familiar mix of mischief and wisdom. "Why don't you start at the beginning, dear? Sometimes, speaking things aloud can help us see what we've missed."

I nod, sinking into the chair across from her. As I recount my conversations with Maggie and Rhonda, Granny listens intently, her ghostly brow furrowed in concentration. When I finish, she's silent for a long moment, her fingers tapping soundlessly on the arm of the chair.

"It seems to me," she says finally, "that you're looking at the pieces of the puzzle, but not the whole picture. This isn't just about a baking competition gone wrong, Lena. There could be something deeper here, something from the past that's come back to haunt poor Arnold."

I lean forward, intrigued. "What do you mean, Granny? Do you know something about Arnold's past?"

Her form flickers slightly, as it often does when she's delving into old memories. "Not much, mind you. But I do remember a scandal, oh, it must have been thirty years ago now. Arnold was just starting out in the baking world, trying to make a name for himself."

My curiosity is piqued. In all the years I've known Arnold, I've never heard about any scandal. "What happened?"

Granny's eyes take on a faraway look. "It was something to do with a business deal, if I remember correctly. Arnold had partnered with someone—I can't recall who—on some sort of baking venture. But it all went south, and there were whispers of fraud, of people losing their life savings."

I feel a chill run down my spine. Could this be connected to the secret Arnold was planning to reveal? "Did anything ever come of it? Was Arnold charged with something?"

She shakes her head. "No, nothing official. The whole thing was hushed up somehow. But mud sticks, especially in a small town like this. It took Arnold years to rebuild his reputation."

My mind is racing with this new information. Could someone from Arnold's past have come back for revenge? Or was Arnold planning to come clean about what really happened all those years ago?

"Granny," I say slowly, "do you think this old scandal could be connected to what happened at the bake-off?"

She fixes me with a piercing gaze. "In my experience, Lena, the past and the present are always connected. We just don't always see the threads that bind them."

I nod, my detective instincts kicking into high gear. "I need to look into this. If there's a connection, it could be the key to solving Arnold's murder."

She smiles approvingly. "That's my girl. But remember, Lena, digging up the past can be dangerous. People will go to great lengths to keep their secrets buried."

With Granny's warning ringing in my ears, I head to my study, firing up my laptop. If there's any record of this old scandal, I'm determined to find it. Hours pass as I comb through online archives, old newspaper clippings, and public records. My eyes burn from staring at the screen, but I push on, fueled by the sense that I'm on the verge of a breakthrough.

And then, just as I'm about to call it quits, I find it. A small article from a regional business journal, dated 1994. The headline reads: "Local Bakery Closes Amid Fraud Allegations."

My heart pounding, I scan the article. It doesn't mention Arnold by name, but it talks about a family-owned bakery in New Oslo that went under after a failed expansion attempt. The details are vague, but there are hints of financial impropriety, of investors losing money.

I sit back, my mind whirling. Could this be the bakery Granny was talking about? And if so, was Arnold really involved in the alleged fraud?

As if summoned by my thoughts, Granny's ghostly form appears beside me. "You've found something," she says. It's not a question.

I nod, gesturing to the screen. "A bakery that went under in '94. It fits with what you told me, but I don't see how it's connected to Arnold."

Granny leans in, her spectral form passing partly through my shoulder. I suppress a shiver at the cold sensation. "Ah," she says softly. "I remember now. It wasn't just any bakery, Lena. It was Arnold's family business."

The pieces start to fall into place. "Arnold's family owned a bakery? But I thought he was always just a judge, never a baker himself."

Granny nods, her expression somber. "The bakery was his parents' dream. Arnold worked there as a young man, but his heart was never in it. He wanted bigger things, to be part of the wider baking world. When his parents retired, he took over, but..."

"But it failed," I finish. "And not just failed, but went down in scandal."

"Exactly," Ingrid says. "It nearly ruined the family. Arnold's parents lost everything - their business, their savings, their home. It's why Arnold threw himself into judging competitions. He was trying to rebuild, to make amends in the only way he knew how."

I lean back in my chair, processing this new information. "But what about Grant? Arnold's son? He must have been just a kid when all this happened."

Granny's eyes take on a sad, faraway look. "Ah, yes. Grant. He would have been, what, ten or eleven at the time? Old enough to understand that something bad had happened, but too young to really grasp why."

A thought strikes me. "Granny, do you think this could be why Grant and Arnold were estranged? Maybe Grant blamed his father for what happened to the family?"

Ingrid nods slowly. "It's certainly possible. Childhood trauma like that can leave deep scars. And if Grant ever found out the full story of what happened..."

She trails off, but I can fill in the blanks. If Grant discovered that his father had been involved in something fraudulent, something that destroyed not just their family but others as well, it could easily have driven a wedge between them.

"But what does all this have to do with the bake-off?" I muse aloud. "Why would something that happened thirty years ago lead to Arnold's murder now?"

Granny fixes me with a piercing gaze. "Think, Lena. What was it that Rhonda said? That Arnold was planning to reveal something that would 'change everything'?"

My eyes widen as the implications hit me. "You think Arnold was going to come clean about what really happened with the bakery? But why now, after all these years?"

She shrugs, her ghostly shoulders shimmering. "Guilt can be a powerful motivator, dear. Perhaps Arnold finally decided it was time to face the consequences of his past actions."

I nod slowly, the pieces starting to come together in my mind. "And if someone else was involved in whatever happened back then, someone who stood to lose everything if the truth came out..."

"They might have been desperate enough to silence Arnold permanently," she finishes grimly.

A chill runs down my spine at the thought. What seemed like a simple case of a local competition gone wrong has suddenly become something much darker, much more complex.

"But who?" I wonder aloud. "Who else could have been involved? And how does this connect to Maggie, Rhonda, and the others?"

Granny's form starts to fade, a sign that her energy is waning. "Trust your instincts, Lena," she says, her voice growing fainter. "You have all the pieces. You just need to see how they fit together."

As she disappears completely, I'm left alone with my thoughts and the weight of this new information. The old family scandal, the failed bakery, the rift between Arnold and Grant - it all has to be connected to what happened at the Bake-Off. But how?

I stand up, stretching my stiff muscles, and move to the window. The sun is setting over New Oslo, casting long shadows across the quiet streets. Somewhere out there, a killer is walking free, perhaps thinking they've gotten away with silencing Arnold forever.

But they didn't count on me. They didn't count on a determined amateur sleuth with a ghostly grandmother and a burning desire for the truth.

Chapter 9

It's way too early in the morning as I make my way down the winding path to Grant McCarthy's cabin, but—as Granny is fond of saying—it's the early bird that catches the worm.

Probably because the worm is still half-asleep.

Still, I have a feeling it's going to be a long day, and what better way to spend the first part of it than by hiking out to the middle of nowhere to visit someone I hardly know?

Grant's cabin is a small, weathered structure on the outskirts of town, nestled among towering pines that seem to whisper secrets in the early morning breeze. As I approach, I can't help but feel a sense of unease settling in my stomach. After everything I've learned about Arnold's past, this conversation with his estranged son feels more crucial than ever.

I take a second to steel my nerves before knocking on the worn wooden door. For a long moment, there's silence, and I wonder if Grant is even home. Then I hear heavy footsteps, and the door swings open with a creak that seems to echo my own apprehension.

Grant McCarthy stands before me, a imposing figure framed by the doorway. His resemblance to Arnold is striking, but where Arnold's face had always been open and friendly, Grant's is a mask of barely contained anger and bitterness. His eyes, the same shade of blue as his father's, are hard and guarded as they meet mine.

"Miss Larsen," he says in a gruff voice. "I wondered how long it would take you to show up at my door."

I blink, taken aback by his bluntness. "I'm sorry to disturb you so early, Mr. McCarthy. I was hoping we could talk about your father."

A muscle twitches in Grant's jaw, and for a moment, I think he might slam the door in my face. But then he steps back, gesturing for me to enter with a curt nod.

The interior of the cabin is spartan, almost austere. A far cry from the warm, cluttered coziness I remember of Arnold's home. As Grant leads me to a small sitting area, I can't help but notice the lack of personal touches. No family photos, no mementos. It's as if Grant has deliberately erased all traces of his past from this space.

"So," Grant says as we sit, his tone brusque, "what is it you want to know? I've already told the police everything."

I lean forward, trying to project an air of calm understanding. "I know this must be difficult for you, Mr. McCarthy. Losing a parent is never easy, even when relationships are... complicated."

Grant lets out a harsh laugh, the sound devoid of any humor. "Complicated? Is that what you call it when your father destroys your family's legacy and then spends the next three decades pretending nothing happened?"

I feel a chill at his words, remembering what Granny Ingrid had told me about the failed bakery. "You're talking about the family business? The bakery?"

Grant's eyes narrow, a flash of surprise quickly masked by suspicion. "How do you know about that? Has someone been talking to you?"

I choose my words carefully, not wanting to reveal too much about my ghostly source of information. "I've been doing some research into the town's past. I came across some old articles about a bakery that went under about thirty years ago. Your family's bakery."

For a moment, the anger in Grant's eyes is replaced by a deep, raw pain. It's gone in an instant, but it's enough to confirm my suspicions. This isn't just about a failed business venture. For Grant, it's about a childhood destroyed, a family torn apart.

"That bakery was everything to my grandparents," Grant says, his voice low and intense. "They built it from nothing, poured their entire lives into it. And my father... he threw it all away. His grand plans, his 'vision' for expansion. It was all just ego and greed."

I nod sympathetically, encouraging him to continue. "It must have been devastating for you, watching it all fall apart."

Grant's laugh is bitter. "Devastating? I was eleven years old. One day, I'm helping my grandmother frost cupcakes, dreaming about taking over the family business someday. The next, we're packing up our home, watching as everything we owned was sold off to pay my father's debts."

As he speaks, I can almost see the scene he's describing—a young Grant, confused and heartbroken, watching his world crumble around him. It's a poignant image, one that tugs at my heartstrings even as my mind catalogs every detail.

"Is that why you and your father were estranged?" I ask gently. "Because of what happened with the bakery?"

Grant's expression hardens again. "That was part of it. But it was more than that. It was his refusal to take responsibility, his need to control everything and everyone around him. Even after the bakery was gone, he couldn't let go. He had to be the expert, the judge, the one who decided who was worthy and who wasn't."

I lean in, sensing we're getting to the heart of the matter. "And you felt judged by him?"

"Constantly," Grant spits out. "Nothing I did was ever good enough. I couldn't live up to the legacy of a business that didn't even exist anymore. So I left. Built my own life away from his shadow."

As Grant speaks, I can't help but notice the tension in his body, the way his hands clench and unclench. There's more here than just old resentments. There's a current of pain so deep, so raw, that it almost crackles in the air between us.

"Mr. McCarthy," I say carefully, "I have to ask. Given your feelings about your father, about what happened... were you involved in his death?"

The question hangs in the air for a long moment. It's a risk to ask something so blunt and straightforward, but these are just the types of conversations that sometimes yield the surprising truth. Grant's eyes meet mine, and I see a whirlwind of emotions there—anger, pain, and something else. Fear?

"No," he says finally, his voice firm. "I didn't kill my father. I hated what he did to our family, yes. I resented his controlling nature, his refusal to acknowledge his mistakes. But I would never... I'm not a murderer, Miss Larsen."

I nod, studying his face carefully. There's a ring of truth to his words, but I can't shake the feeling that he's holding something back. "I believe you, Mr. McCarthy. But is there anything else you can tell me? Anything that might help us understand why someone would want to harm your father?"

Grant is silent for a long moment, his gaze fixed on some point in the distance. When he finally speaks, his voice is softer, tinged with a sadness that seems to age him before my eyes.

"My father... he wasn't an evil man. Not even a bad man. Just a proud one. Too proud to admit when he was wrong, too stubborn to ask for help when he needed it. The bakery... it wasn't entirely his fault. There were others involved, people who took advantage of his inexperience, his desire to make something grand."

I lean forward, my heart racing. This is new information, something that could potentially blow the case wide open. "Others? Do you know who?"

But Grant shakes his head, the shutters coming down over his eyes once more. "No names. It was all hushed up, swept under the rug. But the damage was done. To our family, to others who lost money in the venture. My father spent the rest of his life trying to make amends in his own way, but... some debts can't be repaid with blue ribbons and trophies."

As I process this new information, a thought strikes me. "Mr. McCarthy, do you know Rhonda Peterson? The runner-up in the Bake-Off?"

The change in Grant's demeanor is subtle but unmistakable. A slight tensing of his shoulders, a flicker of... something in his eyes. Protectiveness? "Rhonda? Yes, I know her. She's... a friend. Why do you ask?"

I keep my tone casual, even as my mind races with the implications. "I spoke with her the other day. She seemed very upset about your father's death. I just wondered if you knew why she might have been so affected."

Grant's response is immediate and defensive. "Rhonda's a kind person. Of course she'd be upset about a murder in our community. And she worked closely with my father on the Bake-Off committee. It's natural that she'd be shaken."

But there's something in the way he says it, a forced casualness that doesn't quite ring true. I file this information away for later consideration, sensing that there's more to the connection between Grant and Rhonda than he's letting on.

As our conversation winds down, I find myself more confused than ever. Grant's anger and bitterness towards his father are palpable, but so is his pain. And beneath it all, there's a current of protectiveness—toward the memory of his grandparents, towards Rhonda, and perhaps even, in some complicated way, toward Arnold himself.

I stand to leave, thanking Grant for his time. As I reach the door, he calls out, stopping me.

"Miss Larsen," he says, his voice gruff but not unkind, "be careful where you dig. The past... it has a way of hurting people in the present. Sometimes it's better to let sleeping dogs lie."

I turn back to him, struck by the weariness in his eyes. "Even if it means a murderer goes free?"

Grant's smile is sad, almost pitying. "In my experience, the truth rarely sets anyone free. It just creates new prisons."

As I make my way back down the winding path, Grant's words echo in my mind. The morning sun has fully risen now, casting long shadows through the trees. I can't help but feel that those shadows are a perfect metaphor for this case—the long reach of the past, darkening the present in ways I'm only beginning to understand.

Chapter 10

I'm strolling through Maple Grove Park, my mind churning with all the pieces of this puzzling case, when I spot a familiar figure in the distance. Betty O'Connor sits alone on a weathered wooden bench, tossing breadcrumbs to a flock of eager pigeons. Even from here, I can see the tense set of her shoulders, the angry furrow of her brow as she scatters food with sharp, aggressive motions.

For a moment, I consider turning back. Betty's sharp tongue and competitive nature are well-known in New Oslo, and approaching her now, when she's clearly in a foul mood, seems unwise. But then I steel myself. If I want to get to the bottom of Arnold's murder, I can't shy away from difficult conversations.

As I approach, the crunch of gravel under my feet alerts Betty to my presence. She looks up, her eyes narrowing as she recognizes me. The pigeons scatter in a flutter of wings, startled by her sudden movement.

"Well, well," she says, her voice dripping with sarcasm. "If it isn't our local Nancy Drew. Come to interrogate me too, have you?"

I force a smile, trying to keep my tone light as I gesture to the empty space beside her. "Hello, Betty. Mind if I join you? I was hoping we could talk for a few minutes. About the Bake-Off, and... what happened."

Betty's laugh is sharp, almost bitter. "Oh, I bet you were. Everyone's talking, aren't they? Poor Arnold, murdered right there in front of everyone. And now here you are, playing detective." She pats the bench beside her with exaggerated politeness. "By all means, sit. Tell me, Lena, do you think you can solve what the police can't?"

I settle onto the bench, meeting her gaze steadily and refusing to be intimidated. "I'm just trying to understand what happened, Betty. You've been part of the Bake-Off for years. I thought you might have some insights."

Betty studies me for a long moment, then sighs, tossing another handful of breadcrumbs to the cautiously returning pigeons. "Fine. But make it quick. Unlike some people, I actually have things to do."

Debatable, since we're both sitting here on this park bench and she's idly feeding the birds, but I think it's probably best if I leave that point alone.

As we sit there, surrounded by the gentle cooing of pigeons and the distant laughter of children on the playground, I decide to start with something simple, hoping to put her at ease.

"You've competed against Maggie Fields many times over the years, haven't you?" I ask.

Betty's response is immediate and vehement. "Competed against her? Ha! That's a polite way of putting it. I've watched that woman scheme and connive her way through every competition for the past decade."

I lean forward, intrigued by the venom in Betty's voice. "What do you mean, scheme and connive? Are you saying Maggie cheats?"

Betty's eyes flash with a mixture of anger and what almost looks like triumph. She crushes a piece of bread in her fist, scattering the crumbs with more force than necessary. "I'm saying that Maggie Fields has never won a competition fair and square in her life. Oh, she's clever about it, I'll give her that.

Always just on the right side of the rules, but pushing every boundary."

I nod, encouraging her to continue. "And this year's Bake-Off? Do you think she did something... underhanded to win?"

Betty leans in, her voice dropping to a conspiratorial whisper, as if afraid the pigeons might overhear. "I know she did. You want to know something interesting, Lena? I saw Maggie talking to Arnold before the festival started. They were off by the oak trees over there, speaking in hushed tones. And Arnold... he looked worried."

My heart rate picks up at this new piece of information. Could this be connected to the secret Arnold was planning to reveal? "Did you hear what they were saying?"

Betty shakes her head, frustration evident in her expression. "No, they were too far away. But I know Maggie. That woman always has an angle, always working some scheme. I wouldn't be surprised if she was trying to influence the judging somehow."

I consider this for a moment, watching a bold pigeon hop closer to peck at the crumbs near our feet. "That's a serious accusation, Betty. Do you have any proof?"

Betty's laugh is harsh, scaring away the nearby birds. "Proof? Of course not. Maggie's too smart for that. But mark my words, that blue ribbon she's so proud of? It's as fake as her 'homemade' pie crust."

As Betty speaks, I can't help but notice the depth of her resentment towards Maggie. It seems to go beyond mere rivalry, beyond even the bitterness of losing. There's something personal here, a grudge that feels older and deeper than a simple baking competition.

"Betty," I say carefully, watching her agitated movements as she continues to scatter bread, "I have to ask. Your dislike for Maggie... it seems very intense. Is there more to it than just the competition?"

She turns away, staring out over the park. "More to it? Isn't that enough? Year after year, watching her swan in with her store-bought pies and her false modesty, trying to fool everyone. Do you know what it's like, Lena, to work your fingers to the bone, to pour your heart and soul into something, only to have it snatched away by a cheat?"

I nod sympathetically, even as my mind races. Betty's anger is real, that much is clear. But is it enough to drive her to murder? "I understand your frustration, Betty. But... Arnold's death. Do you think it could be connected to the competition? To Maggie's win?"

Betty's expression turns guarded. She looks around the park, as if suddenly aware of how public our conversation is. "Connected? I don't know about that. Murder is... well, it's a far cry from cheating at a baking contest, isn't it?"

I watch her carefully, noting the way her hands twist the empty bread bag, the nervous dart of her eyes. "But if someone thought Arnold was going to expose some sort of cheating or fraud..."

"Then they'd have more to worry about than losing a blue ribbon," Betty finishes, her voice grim. She leans back on the bench, fixing me with a hard stare. "Listen, Lena. I may not like Maggie Fields. I may think she's a lying, cheating piece of work. But murder? That's... that's something else entirely."

I nod, processing this. A jogger passes by, momentarily distracting us both. When I turn back to Betty, I decide to change tack. "What about Rhonda? You've competed against her too, right? What do you think of her?"

At the mention of Rhonda's name, Betty's expression shifts, becoming almost pitying. "Rhonda? Oh, she's harmless enough. Always the bridesmaid, never the bride, if you know what I mean. Although..." She trails off, a thoughtful look crossing her face.

"Although what?" I prompt.

Betty shakes her head, as if clearing away a stray thought. "Nothing. Just... well, Rhonda's been acting odd lately. Jumpy. Like she's carrying around some big secret. But then again, we're all on edge after what happened, aren't we?"

I file this information away, adding it to the growing puzzle in my mind. "Betty," I say, deciding to take a risk, "if you know anything—anything at all—that might help figure out what happened to Arnold, you need to come forward."

Betty's laugh is sharp and humorless, echoing across the park. "Come forward? To who? The police? Please. They've already made up their minds that it was some random act of violence. And you..." She fixes me with a piercing stare. "You're not a detective, Lena. You're a busybody with more curiosity than sense."

I feel a flash of anger at her words, but I force myself to remain calm. "I'm just trying to find the truth, Betty. For Arnold's sake, and for the town's."

Betty's expression softens, just a fraction. "I know you are, honey. And that's admirable, in its way. But let me give you a piece of advice—be careful. You start poking around in other people's business, asking questions about things that don't concern you... well, you might not like what you find."

There's something in her tone that sends a chill down my spine, despite the warmth of the day. "Are you threatening me, Betty?"

She stands up, brushing breadcrumbs from her skirt. "Threatening? Oh no, dear. I'm warning you. As one citizen of New Oslo to another. Some secrets are buried deep for a reason. And some people... well, they'll do anything to keep those secrets buried."

As I gather my things to leave, Betty's voice stops me. "Oh, and Lena? One more thing. Be careful about getting too close to Maggie or Rhonda. Those two... there's more going on there than meets the eye."

I turn back to her, intrigued. "What do you mean?"

But Betty just shakes her head, already turning to walk away. "Just be careful, that's all I'm saying. In a small town like this, everyone has secrets. And some of them are downright deadly."

As I watch Betty's retreating figure, my mind is whirling with everything I've learned—and everything I still don't know. Betty's obvious hatred for Maggie, her cryptic warnings about Rhonda, the implication that there's more to their rivalry than just a baking competition... it all adds another layer of complexity to an already convoluted case.

I start walking along the park path, my thoughts racing. Betty's animosity toward Maggie seems to run deeper than mere professional jealousy. There's a personal edge to it, a bitterness that speaks of old wounds and long-held grudges. But is it enough to drive someone to murder?

And what about her warnings regarding Maggie and Rhonda? What secrets could they be hiding? I think back to my conversations with both women, trying to piece together a coherent picture. Maggie's nervousness, Rhonda's evasiveness, the hidden ribbons, the hushed conversations... there's a pattern here, I'm sure of it. But what does it all mean?

As I walk, I can't shake the feeling that I'm missing something crucial. Some vital piece of the puzzle that would make everything click into place. The old scandal with Arnold's bakery, the current rivalries in the Bake-Off, the secret Arnold was planning to reveal... they're all connected somehow. I just need to figure out how.

Chapter 11

I pace back and forth in my living room, the floorboards creaking beneath my feet in a rhythm that matches the racing of my thoughts. The wall in front of me is covered in notes, photos, and red string connecting various pieces of evidence—and I'm struggling to piece it all together.

"You're going to wear a hole in that floor if you keep that up," Granny Ingrid's spectral voice chimes in. She's perched on her favorite armchair, her ghostly form shimmering slightly in the afternoon light.

"I can't help it, Granny. I feel like I'm so close to figuring this out, but there's still something missing."

The doorbell rings, interrupting my train of thought. It's Charlie, right on time. I let her in, and she whistles low as she takes in the evidence wall.

"Wow, Lena," she says, eyes wide. "You've been busy."

I nod, grateful for her presence. Charlie has always been my sounding board, the one person besides Granny who truly understands how my mind works.

"Okay," I say, taking a deep breath. "Let's go through this one more time."

For the next hour, we pore over every piece of evidence, every conversation, every hunch. Charlie and Granny listen intently, offering insights and asking questions that force me to look at things from new angles.

"So, we know Arnold had a secret he was planning to reveal," Charlie says, tapping a photo of the deceased judge. "And we assumed it was related to the bake-off, right?"

I nod, but something in her tone makes me pause. "You don't think it was?"

She shrugs. "I don't know. It's just... everyone we've talked to has been so focused on the competition. What if that's what's throwing us off?"

Granny Ingrid leans forward, her ghostly eyes sparkling. "Your friend is onto something, Lena. Remember what I always taught you—when everyone's looking in one direction, that's when you should look the other way."

I feel a tingle of excitement run down my spine. "You're right. We've been so caught up in the bake-off angle, we might have missed something obvious."

I turn back to the wall, my eyes scanning over the information with renewed focus. Suddenly, a pattern begins to emerge—one I can't believe I didn't see before.

"Rhonda," I breathe. "It all comes back to Rhonda."

Charlie and Granny exchange a look. "What do you mean?" Charlie asks.

I start pointing to various notes and photos. "Look. Rhonda was acting nervous, more upset about Arnold's death than seemed warranted for just a colleague. Grant was protective of her when I mentioned her name. And Betty... Betty said Rhonda was carrying around some big secret."

The pieces start falling into place with dizzying speed. "Arnold's secret wasn't about the Bake-Off at all," I say, my voice rising with excitement. "It was about an affair—with Rhonda!"

Granny Ingrid claps her spectral hands. "Oh, well done, dear! That does explain quite a bit, doesn't it?"

Charlie nods slowly, her brow furrowed in thought. "But if the secret was about an affair, why kill Arnold? Surely that would just bring more attention to it?"

I shake my head, the final pieces of the puzzle clicking into place. "Because Rhonda panicked. Think about it—small town like New Oslo, a scandal like that could ruin her. Her business, her reputation, everything she's worked for."

"But what about Maggie?" Charlie asks. "Where does she fit into all this?"

I turn back to the wall, my finger landing on a photo of the blue ribbon winner. "Maggie's not innocent in all this. Remember how nervous she was? How defensive? I think... I think she might have bribed Arnold to ensure her win."

Granny Ingrid lets out a low whistle. "My, my. Bribes, affairs, murder... who knew our little baking competition could be so sordid?"

I nod grimly. "Maggie bribed Arnold, probably threatened to expose the affair if he didn't comply. But then Arnold decided to come clean about everything—the bribe, the affair, all of it."

"And Rhonda killed him to keep it quiet," Charlie finishes, his voice hushed.

The weight of the truth settles over the room. We've solved the mystery, but there's no joy in the revelation—only a deep sadness for the web of lies and desperation that led to this tragedy.

"So what now?" Charlie asks after a moment of heavy silence.

I take a deep breath, squaring my shoulders. "Now, we bring this to light. We owe it to Arnold, to the town. The truth needs to come out."

Granny Ingrid nods approvingly. "Well said, dear. But be careful. Cornered animals are the most dangerous, and you're about to corner two of them."

Charlie's eyes widen. "Lena, you can't confront them alone. It's too dangerous."

I shake my head, a plan already forming. "Not alone, and not in private. We need to do this somewhere public, somewhere they can't easily escape or..." I trail off, not wanting to voice the darker possibilities.

"The town council meeting," Charlie says suddenly. "It's tonight. Everyone will be there, especially after the murder. You know how this town loves its gossip."

I feel a smile spread across my face. "Charlie, you're a genius. It's perfect. Public enough to be safe, but official enough to be taken seriously. Plus, Sheriff Mark will be there."

Granny Ingrid nods approvingly. "A sound plan. But you'll need to be careful about how you approach this, Lena. You don't want to spook them before you can get the truth out."

For the next hour, we strategize. Charlie helps me organize my evidence and prepare what I'm going to say. Granny Ingrid offers advice on reading people's reactions and staying calm under pressure.

As the time for the meeting approaches, I feel a mix of nerves and determination. This is it—the moment of truth. One way or another, by the end of this night, the truth will come out.

"Ready?" Charlie asks as we prepare to leave.

I take a deep breath, nodding. "As I'll ever be."

Granny Ingrid's voice floats after us as we head out the door. "Remember, Lena—the truth is on your side. Trust in that, and in yourself."

With those words bolstering my courage, I step out into the evening, ready to bring New Oslo's darkest secrets into the light.

The town hall is buzzing with activity as Charlie and I arrive. It seems like half of New Oslo has turned out for this meeting, no doubt eager for any new gossip about Arnold's murder. I spot familiar faces everywhere—Mrs. Landry from the post office, old Mr. Finch who runs the hardware store, even my third-grade teacher, Mrs. Abernathy.

As we make our way to some empty seats near the front, I catch sight of Sheriff Mark. Our eyes meet, and I see a flicker of concern cross his face. He knows me well enough to recognize when I'm up to something.

My heart races as I scan the room, quickly locating both Maggie and Rhonda. They're sitting on opposite sides of the hall, each looking tense and uncomfortable. Neither of them notices me, too wrapped up in their own thoughts and worries.

Mayor Thompson calls the meeting to order, his gavel echoing through the packed room. "Before we begin with our regular agenda," he announces, "I'd like to address the tragic event that has shaken our community. Sheriff Mark will give us an update on the investigation into Arnold McCarthy's murder."

As Mark steps up to the podium, I feel a moment of doubt. Am I really about to do this? To accuse two respected members of the community of bribery and murder? But then I think of Arnold, of the truth he was prepared to reveal, and my resolve hardens.

Mark's update is brief and uninformative—clearly, the police are still grasping at straws. As he steps down, I see my opportunity.

"Excuse me, Mayor Thompson," I say, standing up. My voice comes out steadier than I feel. "If I may, I have some information relevant to Arnold's death that I believe the town should hear."

A murmur ripples through the crowd. I can feel all eyes on me, including the sharp, concerned gaze of Sheriff Mark. Mayor Thompson looks flustered but nods. "Very well, Ms. Larsen. The floor is yours."

As I make my way to the front of the room, I catch sight of Maggie and Rhonda. Maggie has gone pale, her hands gripping the edge of her seat. Rhonda looks like she might be sick.

I take a deep breath, steeling myself. "Thank you, Mayor. What I'm about to say may come as a shock to many of you, but I believe it's the truth behind Arnold McCarthy's murder."

The room falls deadly silent. I can almost hear the collective intake of breath as everyone leans forward, eager for the revelation.

"First," I say, my eyes finding Maggie in the crowd, "I need to address Maggie Fields."

Maggie's eyes widen, a deer-in-headlights look that confirms my suspicions. "Maggie," I continue, keeping my voice calm but firm, "you won this year's Bake-Off. But it wasn't a fair win, was it?"

A gasp ripples through the crowd. Maggie stands up, her face a mask of indignation. "How dare you! I worked hard for that win!"

I nod, acknowledging her words. "You did work hard, Maggie. But you also hedged your bets, didn't you? You bribed Arnold to ensure your victory."

The room erupts in shocked whispers. Maggie's face crumples, the fight going out of her. "I... I didn't... It wasn't like that," she stammers.

"Tell the truth, Maggie," I press gently. "Arnold was going to reveal everything. That's why you were so nervous when I talked to you."

Tears well up in Maggie's eyes. "I just... I wanted to win so badly. You don't understand what it's like, always coming in second. I offered Arnold money to... to look favorably on my entry. But I swear, I didn't kill him! When I heard he was going to confess, I was relieved. I was going to come clean too."

A collective gasp echoes through the town hall. I nod, feeling a pang of sympathy for Maggie despite everything. "Thank you for your honesty, Maggie."

But this is only the first part of the truth. The harder part is yet to come. I turn, my eyes finding Rhonda in the crowd. She's shrunk down in her seat, her face ashen.

"Rhonda," I say softly. "Arnold's secret wasn't just about the bribe, was it?"

Rhonda shakes her head frantically, her eyes darting around the room like a trapped animal. "I don't know what you're talking about," she says, her voice high and panicky.

"I think you do," I press on, my heart pounding. "Arnold was going to reveal everything—including your affair."

The room explodes into chaos. Sheriff Mark steps forward, his face a mix of shock and dawning comprehension. "Lena, what are you saying?"

I keep my eyes on Rhonda, watching as the last of her composure crumbles. "Arnold and Rhonda were having an affair.

But it was more than that, wasn't it, Rhonda? You were in love with him."

Rhonda lets out a choked sob, her whole body shaking. "You don't understand," she whispers. "None of you understand."

"Help us understand, Rhonda," I say gently. "Tell us what happened."

And suddenly, like a dam bursting, the words pour out of Rhonda. "I loved him. We were going to be together, finally. But then... then he said he was going to tell everyone. About us, about Maggie's bribe, everything. He said it was the right thing to do."

Tears stream down Rhonda's face as she continues, her voice barely above a whisper. "I begged him not to. My business, my life in this town—it would all be over. But he wouldn't listen. He said the truth had to come out."

The room is silent now, everyone hanging on Rhonda's every word. I can see the moment she breaks, the last of her resistance crumbling away.

"I didn't mean to," she sobs. "I just... I panicked. I saw the knife there, and I... oh God, what have I done?"

Sheriff Mark steps forward, his face grim. "Rhonda Peterson, I'm placing you under arrest for the murder of Arnold McCarthy."

As Mark leads a sobbing Rhonda away, the room erupts into chaos. People are shouting, crying, demanding answers. Mayor Thompson bangs his gavel frantically, trying to restore order.

I sink back into my seat, feeling drained. Charlie puts a comforting hand on my shoulder. "You did it, Lena," she says softly. "You found the truth."

But as I look around at the shocked and tearful faces of my neighbors, at Maggie being consoled by Betty of all people, at the empty spaces where Rhonda and Arnold should be, I don't feel triumphant. I feel sad. Sad for Arnold, for Rhonda, for a town that will never be quite the same.

As the meeting breaks up, people filing out in shocked silence or huddled groups, Sheriff Mark makes his way over to me.

"Lena," he says, his voice a mix of admiration and exasperation, "I don't know whether to thank you or scold you."

I manage a weak smile. "How about we settle for a cup of coffee and a full debrief?"

Mark nods, a small smile tugging at his lips. "Deal. But Lena... next time, maybe give me a heads up before you solve a murder in front of the entire town?"

I laugh, feeling some of the tension of the night finally start to ease. "Where's the fun in that?"

As we walk out into the cool night air, I can't help but feel that this is both an ending and a beginning. The mystery is solved, the truth revealed. But for New Oslo, and for me, I suspect the repercussions of this night will be felt for a long time to come.

But that, I suppose, is a mystery for another day.

Chapter 12

The morning after the town council meeting, I find myself sitting at my kitchen table, a steaming mug of coffee cradled in my hands. The events of the past few days play through my mind like a movie reel, each scene clicking into place with a clarity that had eluded me during the investigation.

It's funny how the truth can be so obvious in hindsight. The nervousness in Rhonda's eyes, the protective edge in Grant's voice when he spoke of her, the hidden meaning behind Betty's cryptic warnings—all the pieces were there, waiting for me to put them together.

I take a sip of my coffee, letting the warmth spread through me. The case is officially closed now. Rhonda's confession, tearful and broken as it was, left no room for doubt. Arnold McCarthy's murder has been solved, the truth laid bare for all of New Oslo to see.

But as I sit here, in the quiet of my kitchen, I can't help but feel a mix of emotions. There's satisfaction, yes—the puzzle-solver in me pleased at having unraveled the mystery. But there's also a deep sadness. For Arnold, whose life was cut short just as he was finding the courage to face his mistakes. For Rhonda, whose desperation and fear led her down a path she can never fully come back from. Even for Maggie, whose desire to win pushed her to compromise her integrity.

The truth, I'm learning, is rarely simple or painless. It's complex and messy, filled with shades of gray that defy easy categorization.

A knock at the door pulls me from my musings. It's Mark, looking tired but determined. I invite him in, pouring him a cup of coffee as he settles into a chair across from me.

"How are you holding up?" he asks, his voice gentle.

I shrug, offering a small smile. "I'm okay. It's all still sinking in, I guess. How about you? I imagine you've had a busy night."

Mark nods, taking a long sip of his coffee. "That's an understatement. Rhonda's been formally charged. Maggie's under investigation for the bribe. The DA's office is having a field day."

We sit in companionable silence for a moment, each lost in our own thoughts. Finally, Mark speaks again, his tone a mix of frustration and admiration.

"You know, Lena, I meant it last night when I said I didn't know whether to thank you or lecture you," he says, a rueful smile playing at his lips. "What you did was incredibly risky. You could have compromised the entire investigation."

I start to protest, but he holds up a hand, stopping me. "But," he continues, "I can't deny that your methods got results. Results that we might never have achieved through official channels."

I feel a warmth spread through me at his words, a mix of pride and something else—something that has more to do with the man sitting across from me than with solving the case.

"So, what you're saying is, you're impressed with my detective skills?" I tease, trying to lighten the mood.

Mark laughs, the sound chasing away some of the tension that's been hanging between us. "I'm saying that you're either the best thing that's ever happened to law enforcement in New Oslo, or the worst. I haven't quite decided which yet."

I grin, raising my mug in a mock toast. "How about we settle on 'unconventional but effective'?"

"I can live with that," Mark agrees, clinking his mug against mine. His expression turns more serious as he adds, "But Lena, promise me something. Next time—because I have a feeling there will be a next time—come to me first. We can work together. It'll be safer for you, and frankly, it'll save me a lot of paperwork."

I nod, touched by the concern in his voice. "Deal. Partners in crime-solving?"

"Partners," he agrees, and the way he says it makes me think he might be considering a partnership that extends beyond just solving mysteries.

As if reading my mind, Mark clears his throat, a hint of nervousness creeping into his voice. "So, uh, about that date we never got to finish... I was thinking, maybe once the dust settles a bit, we could try again?"

I feel a flutter in my stomach, a spark of excitement that has nothing to do with mysteries or murders. "I'd like that," I say softly. "I'd like that a lot."

Mark's smile is like the sun breaking through clouds, warm and full of promise. As he leaves to head back to the station, I find myself standing in the doorway, watching him go with a lightness in my heart that I haven't felt in days.

"Well, well," a familiar spectral voice chimes in. "Looks like solving murders isn't the only thing you're good at, dear."

I turn to see Granny Ingrid's ghostly form shimmering into view, a mischievous twinkle in her eye.

"Granny," I say, feeling a rush of affection for my spectral mentor. "I was wondering when you'd show up."

She settles into her favorite armchair. "Oh, I've been around. Didn't want to interrupt your little tête-à-tête with the handsome sheriff."

I feel a blush creeping up my cheeks. "It wasn't... we were just discussing the case."

"Mhmm," Granny hums, clearly unconvinced. "And I suppose that twinkle in your eye is just from the thrill of solving the mystery?"

I laugh, unable to keep up the pretense. "Okay, okay. Maybe there's a little more to it than that."

Granny's expression softens, a look of pride and love shining in her ghostly eyes. "I'm happy for you, dear. And not just about the sheriff. You did good with this case. Real good."

Her words warm me more than any cup of coffee could. "Thanks, Granny. I couldn't have done it without you, you know."

She waves off my gratitude with a transparent hand. "Nonsense. You've got all the makings of a first-rate detective, Lena. You just needed a little nudge in the right direction now and then."

We sit in comfortable silence for a while, each lost in our own thoughts. Outside, I can hear the town coming to life. Car doors slamming, voices calling out greetings, the distant chime of the church bells. Life in New Oslo goes on, despite the shocking revelations of the past few days.

"They'll be talking about this for months, you know," Granny says, echoing my thoughts. "Nothing like a good scandal to get the gossip mill churning."

I nod, feeling a mix of emotions at the thought. "I know. Part of me wishes we could have solved this without airing everyone's dirty laundry in public. But..."

"But the truth needed to come out," Granny finishes for me. "For Arnold's sake, and for the town's."

"Exactly," I agree. "I just hope that eventually, people will be able to move past the gossip and remember Arnold for who he was, not just how he died."

Granny's ghostly hand reaches out, passing through my arm in what I know is meant to be a comforting gesture. "They will, dear. Time has a way of putting things in perspective. And who knows? Maybe some good will come out of all this. Maybe people will be a little kinder, a little more honest with each other."

I smile at her optimism, feeling some of my own hope rekindled. "Maybe you're right, Granny. Maybe this is a chance for New Oslo to start fresh."

As the day wears on, I find myself drawn to my front porch. I settle into the old rocking chair, watching as the sun begins its descent towards the horizon. The sky is a painter's palette of oranges and pinks, a beautiful end to a tumultuous few days.

From my perch, I can see much of the town. The steeple of the church, the roof of the town hall, the distant glimmer of the lake. It all looks so peaceful, so ordinary. And yet, I know that beneath the surface, New Oslo is buzzing with the aftermath of Arnold's murder and Rhonda's confession.

I can almost hear the conversations happening behind closed doors, over garden fences, in the aisles of the grocery store. The shock, the sadness, the inevitable questions of "How could we not have known?" and "What if...?"

But mixed in with the gossip and the second-guessing, I hope there's also reflection. On the nature of truth and lies, on the weight of secrets, on the consequences of our actions. Maybe, just maybe, this tragedy will lead to some soul-searching, some healing.

As for me, I feel a sense of peace settling over me. Justice has been served, however imperfectly. The truth is out, for better or worse. And while I know the ripple effects of this case will be felt for a long time to come, I also know that New Oslo is resilient. We'll weather this storm, just as we've weathered others before.

My thoughts drift to Mark, to the promise of our upcoming date. Despite everything that's happened—or maybe because of it—I find myself looking forward to exploring this new dimension of our relationship. There's something exciting about the prospect of getting to know him not just as the town sheriff, but as Mark—the man behind the badge.

And yet, even as I allow myself to daydream about romantic possibilities, I can feel the stirring of my detective instincts. Because I know that even with this case solved, there will always be more mysteries in New Oslo. More secrets waiting to be uncovered, more truths hiding in plain sight.

It's a thought that both thrills and sobers me. I know now, in a way I didn't before, the weight of uncovering those truths. The responsibility that comes with piecing together the puzzle of people's lives and choices.

But I also know that I can't turn away from it. This case has awakened something in me—a desire to seek out the truth, to bring light to the shadows, to help in whatever way I can.

I make a silent promise to myself. To use this gift, this knack for solving mysteries, wisely and well. To seek the truth, but to do so with compassion and understanding.

Because in the end, that's what being a detective—amateur or otherwise—is really about. Not just solving puzzles, but helping people. Bringing closure, justice, and sometimes, if we're lucky, a chance for new beginnings.

Get *Granny's Ghost and the Deadly Dinner Party* HERE[1]!

1. https://www.amazon.com/gp/product/B0DJ7PW47X

Also by Sloane Finley

Death by Dessert Series
Death by Chocolate Cupcake[2]
Death by Devil's Food Cake[3]
Death by Tiramisu[4]

Ghostly Gumshoe Series
Granny's Ghost and the Haunted Homicide[5]
Granny's Ghost and the Poisoned Punch[6]
Granny's Ghost and the Bake-Off Bribe[7]
Granny's Ghost and the Deadly Dinner Party[8]
Granny's Ghost and the Movie Night Murder[9]
Granny's Ghost and the Murdered Medium[10]
Granny's Ghost and the Basement Burial[11]
Granny's Ghost and the Murdered Magician[12]

2. https://www.amazon.com/Death-Chocolate-Cupcake-Dessert-Mystery-ebook/dp/B0DPGS8S8Z
3. https://www.amazon.com/gp/product/B0DR7GTS38
4. https://www.amazon.com/Death-Tiramisu-Dessert-Cozy-Mystery-ebook/dp/B0DY2K7ND3
5. https://www.amazon.com/gp/product/B0DFZR8LV6
6. https://www.amazon.com/gp/product/B0DGNN9QNK
7. https://www.amazon.com/gp/product/B0DHB1CBQL
8. https://www.amazon.com/gp/product/B0DJ7PW47X
9. https://www.amazon.com/gp/product/B0DJQ4R3L1
10. https://www.amazon.com/gp/product/B0DKB6Y47K
11. https://www.amazon.com/gp/product/B0DL3GRP97
12. https://www.amazon.com/gp/product/B0DLVJJJ33

Granny's Ghost and the Deadly Delphinium[13]
Granny's Ghost and the Killer Caroler[14]
Granny's Ghost and the Fatal Fashion Show[15]
Granny's Ghost and the Cook-Off Killer[16]
Granny's Ghost and the Tulip Fest Killer[17]
Granny's Ghost and the One-Hit Wonder[18]
Granny's Ghost and the Backyard Butcher[19]
Ghostly Gumshoe Collection (Books 1 - 3)[20]

Hexed and Vexed Series
Pixies, Lies, and Alibis[21]
Sprites, Snitches, and Stitches[22]
Imps, Curses, and Hearses[23]

---

13. https://www.amazon.com/gp/product/B0DMYJ5RQ6
14. https://www.amazon.com/gp/product/B0DNY9H8YM
15. https://www.amazon.com/gp/product/B0DQHXXW7Z
16. https://www.amazon.com/gp/product/B0DRWFBDK4
17. https://www.amazon.com/Grannys-Killer-Ghostly-Gumshoe-Mysteries-ebook/dp/B0F8YZ7BR3/
18. https://www.amazon.com/gp/product/B0FD4Z66MS
19. https://www.amazon.com/gp/product/B0FHC2211L
20. https://www.amazon.com/Ghostly-Gumshoe-Collection-Paranormal-Mystery-ebook/dp/B0DHPDBYQ9
21. https://www.amazon.com/Pixies-Alibis-Hexed-Vexed-Mystery-ebook/dp/B0DV4ZTDLW
22. https://www.amazon.com/Sprites-Snitches-Stitches-Hexed-Mystery-ebook/dp/B0F25BH5NH
23. https://www.amazon.com/Curses-Hearses-Hexed-Vexed-Mystery-ebook/dp/B0F5KTR8CZ

Fur-ensic Files Series

Fetch Me a Felon[24]

Best in Show, Worst in Murder[25]

Dachshund Dynasty[26]

Fur-ensic Files Complete Collection (Books 1 - 3)[27]

24. https://www.amazon.com/gp/product/B0DFVQMWV5

25. https://www.amazon.com/gp/product/B0DHPWBRFT

26. https://www.amazon.com/gp/product/B0DJG9KWYL

27. https://www.amazon.com/Fur-ensic-Files-Collection-Sloane-Finley-ebook/dp/B0DJZV9ZLZ

www.ingramcontent.com/pod-product-compliance
Ingram Content Group UK Ltd.
Pitfield, Milton Keynes, MK11 3LW, UK
UKHW021013180825
7441UKWH00015B/73

9 798231 003006